'Nielsen treats a heavy subject with a light, optimistic touch'
Toronto Star

Praise for *We Are All Made of Molecules*

'There are many great voices in YA fiction, but Susin Nielsen manages to give us TWO in the same book. I defy you not to fall in love with this book' Phil Earle

'There's so much to love about this story, but what grabbed me most is the humour. Who do I write to to join the Susin Nielsen fan club?' Christopher Paul Curtis

'Susin Nielsen is one of the best writers working today' Susan Juby

'This savvy, insightful take on the modern family makes for nearly nonstop laughs' *Kirkus*, starred review

'A book to fortify readers against bullies and homophobes' *Sunday Times*

'Nielsen deals with some big issues – grief, loss, bullying and homophobia – but anchors the story with terrific warmth and humour. One to make you laugh, cry and read in one sitting' *The Bookseller*

'Snappy and witty. A really fine YA novel' *Telegraph*

'A sheer delight. That next life-affirming book' *Storytellers Inc*

THE
Reluctant
JOURNAL
OF
HENRY K.
LARSEN

THE Reluctant JOURNAL OF HENRY K. LARSEN

A NOVEL BY SUSIN NIELSEN

Andersen Press • London

This edition published in 2016 by
Andersen Press Limited
20 Vauxhall Bridge Road
London SW1V 2SA
www.andersenpress.co.uk

2 4 6 8 10 9 7 5 3 1

First published in 2012 in Canada by Tundra Books,
a division of Penguin Random House Canada Ltd

British Library Cataloguing in Publication Data available.

ISBN 978 1 78344 366 6

Printed and bound in Great Britain by Clays Ltd, St Ives plc

For Göran: Oändligt är vårt äventyr

The Reluctant Journal
of Henry K. Larsen

Friday, January 18

INTRIGUING FACT: The word 'psychology' comes from the Greek word 'psyche.' It means *the study of the mind.*

I don't want anyone to study my mind. That's just creepy. But Dad says I no longer have a choice.

Cecil doesn't look like a psychologist. For one thing, his name is *Cecil*. On his door at the Coastal Health Center, a plastic plaque says DR LEVINE, but when I called him that at our first session, he said, 'Please, call me Cecil.' When I got home, I looked up his name, and do you know what it means? *Dim-sighted or blind.*

Not a good sign.

Cecil has long stringy gray hair, and he uses a scrunchy to pull it back. A scrunchy! Today, at our third session, he was wearing yet another tie-dyed shirt, purple this time. *Hey Cecil*, I wanted to say, *the 60s called. They want their look back!*

He says, 'How does that make you feel?' a lot, like we're on a TV show and not real life. He also says, 'Holy Moly' a lot, as in 'Holy Moly, you're fifteen minutes late, two weeks in a row!'

I suspect Cecil is not the crème de la crème of psychologists. For one thing, he is free. Dad says the Province of British Columbia pays him, but I don't think they pay him very much. His office is tiny and cramped, and the furniture is cheap, chipped, and stained. Also, it looks like he hasn't been able to afford new clothes since 1969.

We haven't talked about IT yet. He tries to steer me there. He asks leading questions. But when he does, I just respond in Robot-Voice: 'I. Do Not Know. What You Mean. Humanoid.' And he backs right off.

Robot-Voice is what landed me here in the first place. After the whole thing with Mom at Christmas, my furies came back, and I started speaking in Robot 24/7. Right through the move to Vancouver, even. The thing about speaking Robot is, it strips emotion out of everything. 'It. Is All. In Monotone.' It helps me. But by the eighth day of Robot-Henry, it was freaking everyone else out, so Dad made my first appointment. And he made me keep it, even after I'd gone back to being plain old Henry.

Cecil tries everything in his limited tool kit to get me to talk about IT. For example, last week I mentioned in passing that I like to write, so today he gave me this notebook. 'I thought you might like a private place to record your thoughts and feelings. Journaling can be quite therapeutic.'

I told him I didn't think 'journaling' was a word. When I got home, I threw the notebook in the garbage.

Then I got it out later, but only because I was bored.

The thing is, Cecil <u>knows</u> all about IT. He had a long talk with my dad before my first session, and I'd bet my

Great Dane poster that he Googled the whole thing after-ward, too. And once he was done reading everything he could find, I bet he wondered why my parents didn't get me into therapy right after IT happened, seven and a half months ago.

Holy Moly! I can imagine him thinking. *What took them so long?*

Saturday, January 19

Pizza for dinner again tonight. That's three nights in a row. I guess you could say it's one of the perks of bachelor life.

We watched *Saturday Night Smash-Up* while we ate. Dad had two slices. I ate the rest. Halfway through dinner, I had to change out of my pants and into my pajama bottoms so my wobblies could have a little more room to breathe.

When *Saturday Night Smash-Up* was over, I asked Dad to measure me. Still five foot three.

Thirteen years old, and I'm still a pygmy.

Midnight

My bedroom smells like curry, thanks to what's-his-head next door.

2:00 a.m.

I can hear Dad snoring.

2:30 a.m.

This journal is stupid.

Monday, January 21

INTRIGUING FACT: Killer whales travel around in pods. Each pod has a distinct set of clicking sounds, whistles, and cries. It helps them stick together.

It works the same in the first year of high school. A bunch of scared kids from a bunch of different elementary schools show up in September, and, within weeks, they form their pods. The jocks join teams; the nerds join clubs, like 'chess' or 'computer'; the stoners find a spot behind some bushes, just off school property.

So when a new kid shows up in January, nobody really notices. They already have their pods. And that suits me just fine. I'm happy to be like Luna, the killer whale that strayed from his pod and swam around by himself for a couple of years, off the coast of Vancouver Island. After all, he seemed pretty content. He had a perfectly good life.

Well. Until he was accidentally chopped to bits by a boat's propeller.

But here's the problem. There's always at least one other kid who is also swimming solo, because none of the pods will let him in.

At Port Salish Secondary, that kid was my brother, Jesse.

At Trafalgar Secondary, that kid is Farley Wong.

I'm pretty sure he picked up my scent the day I started here, two weeks ago. But today he went in for the kill.

'Greetings and welcome to our planet, Earthling,' he said to me this morning, with a thick Chinese accent. I was putting my math book in my locker, which, as luck would have it, is only one door down from his. 'Farley Wong.' He held out his hand.

'Henry,' I replied, skipping my last name. He tried to do an elaborate handshake, but I lost him after the first couple of moves.

'Where did you transfer from?'

'Vancouver Island,' I replied. Best to keep it vague.

'We have three classes together,' he said, counting them on his fingers. 'Enriched Math, Phys Ed, and Enriched English.'

I knew this already, only because he's pretty hard to miss. He's the nerdiest-looking kid I have ever seen.

I know, I know. I'm one to talk. Pop-Pop likes to joke that I have so many freckles, it looks like I got a tan through a screen door. And yes, my hair is red and curly. And yes, I am short. And yes, I have to buy my clothes in 'husky' size, which is a nice word for 'fat'.

But I don't *advertise* my nerdiness. Farley looks like the model for that nerd action figure you can buy in novelty stores. He has thick Coke-bottle glasses. He wears short-sleeved button-up shirts and lines the pockets with *plastic protectors*, so the pens he keeps clipped to them won't leak on his clothes. His pants are always ironed, with a neat crease down the middle. He belts them up high, so the waist stops just under his nipples.

And he carries a briefcase!

'You want to walk to English together?' he said. 'I know a shortcut.' He gazed at me, his magnified eyes full of hope.

I'm not dumb. I knew that being seen with Farley could be like committing social hari-kari. In high school, it's all about first impressions. Just look at what happened to Jesse.

But, on the other hand . . .

Farley is the first kid in seven months to talk to me like I'm a regular human being. So I heard myself say, 'Sure.'

Farley talked the whole way to class about a show called *Battlestar Galactica*.

'I have the entire series on DVD. It's frakking brilliant.' The more he talked, the more bits of spittle formed at the sides of his mouth.

We rounded a corner, and a big guy in jeans that hung well below his bum bumped into Farley, accidentally-on-purpose. I recognized him; his locker is across the hall from mine.

'Nice slacks, Fartley,' he said. Then he kicked me. Not too hard, but still. 'Sorry,' he said. 'I thought it was Kick a Ginger Day.'

'I've seen that episode of *South Park*, too,' I retorted. 'Years ago. Pretty stale joke, don't you think?'

OK. I didn't say that. But I thought it.

'That's Troy Vasic,' Farley said after he'd sauntered away. 'You wanna watch out for him.' He was quiet for the rest of our walk. 'Oh, well,' he said when we reached English class. 'I guess there's a Troy Vasic at every school.'

True, I thought.

But at Jesse's school, his name was Scott Marlin.

Farley latched on to me like a leech for the rest of the day. In the afternoon, we had gym together. I'm not very good at sports, but compared to Farley, I'm an Olympic athlete. He's *awful*. The funny thing is, he doesn't seem to care. We played volleyball, and when he finally managed to hit the ball over the net, he shouted, 'Yes!' even though it was way out-of-bounds.

And guess what? He wore his gym shorts pulled up to his nipples, too.

So, you could say Farley is my first new friend. But it's kind of like the first car you buy. It gets you from A to B, but from the moment you own it, you're constantly dreaming of the day you can get an upgrade.

11:00 p.m.

The water stain on my bedroom ceiling looks like a puffer fish.

1:00 a.m.

I think I'll write a little story about Jesse. Cecil would probably pee in his pants if he knew. But he never will because I will never tell him.

Why Jesse Larsen Was Never Accepted into a Pod

by Henry K. Larsen

The first week of high school at Port Salish Secondary, the new kids did 'bonding activities' with the older kids – bowling parties, pizza parties, that kind of thing. It was the school's way of making them feel welcome. On Friday, each new kid had to get up onstage in the auditorium and say a few words, in front of the *entire school*.

When it was Jesse's turn, he said he liked playing on his PS3, reading manga, and watching the Global Wrestling Federation's *Saturday Night Smash-Up*.

It was a little dorky maybe, but no big deal. So he couldn't figure out why the entire audience was laughing like crazy.

When he left the stage, the principal took him aside and said, 'Jesse Larsen, XYZ.'

'What?'

'XYZ. Examine Your Zipper!'

Jesse looked down. His fly had been unzipped during his entire speech.

Again – no big deal.

Except it was.

Mom had told Jesse the week before that she refused to do any of his laundry unless he put it into the hamper. And Jesse never got around to it. So when he discovered that morning that he was out of clean Y-Fronts, he decided that *no* underwear was better than *dirty* underwear.

That's right. He went to school commando. Meaning, every single kid at Port Salish Secondary didn't see his underwear through his fly.

They saw his you-know-whats: his family jewels, his nuggets, his love spuds. His *balls*.

A kid in the front row took pictures with his phone. I was still in elementary school and didn't have a cell phone, but a lot of kids in my class did. So, along with every other kid in Port Salish and beyond, I saw the photographic evidence within the hour.

The school went into overdrive, of course. 'This is a form of bullying, and we won't tolerate bullying of any kind,' blah-blah-blah.

The photos got taken down pretty fast, at least the ones that were posted on Facebook. But the other stuff – the stuff the grown-ups couldn't see or maybe didn't want to see – had just begun.

Scott Marlin gave Jesse his nickname, the one that stuck through his first two years of high school, until he put an end to it for good.

Ballsack.

For almost two full years, the boy formerly known as Jesse was called Ballsack. Some kids even called him that in front of the teachers, who thought they were calling him Balzac, after some dead French writer.

I'm not saying Jesse didn't have his quirks. Scott would have found other things to tease him about. His zits, which were bad. His obsession with the Global Wrestling Federation. The way he giggled when he got nervous.

But the Ballsack event was the biggie. It was the match that lit the fuse that exploded in our faces last June.

As my Enriched English teacher, Mr Schell, would say: 'That, Henry, is what we call an *inciting incident*.'

I stand corrected. Farley *does* have a pod.

It was lunchtime, and we were at our lockers. Troy was across the hall with a couple of friends. When he closed his locker and turned around, he was wearing a pair of 'nerd' glasses – the dollar-store kind with thick black plastic rims and fake magnified eyeballs stuck on the lenses.

Meaning, they made him look a lot like Farley.

'Hey, guys,' Troy said, trying to imitate Farley's Chinese accent. 'How's it hanging?'

His knuckle-dragging friends cracked up. A couple of girls started to laugh a little, too. You could tell they were trying not to, but it was hard. Troy's impersonation was pretty good.

This was Farley's brilliant comeback: 'So funny I forgot to laugh.'

But nobody else forgot to laugh, because the real Farley sounded a lot like Troy's fake Farley. Even I had to swallow an involuntary snort.

Troy and his friends walked away. From the back, they looked like triplets – their jean legs bunched at the ankles, the waists stopping midway down their butts, their shoulders sloped.

'What a bunch of Neanderthals,' I said as I turned back to Farley. That's when I saw the look on his face.

I knew that look. I'd seen it on Jesse's face lots of times, after he'd had another run-in with Scott. It was a complicated look. Part *I hate Troy*, part *I hate myself*.

'I was born with poor eyesight,' he said. 'It's not like there's anything I can do about it.'

'At least you weren't born with two heads, like this Mexican guy in the 1900s,' I told him as I closed my locker door. 'Or with hypertrichosis.'

'What's hypertrichosis?'

'It's when your body produces crazy amounts of hair, even on your face. You're like a human werewolf.'

Farley peered at me and blinked. 'Why do you know that?'

I didn't know what to say. How to explain that in our family, our idea of fun was to play Balderdash or Cranium. Or that our favorite TV show after the GWF's *Saturday Night Smash-Up* was *Jeopardy!* and that we'd try to answer the questions before the contestants did. Or that our favorite books were *Uncle John's Bathroom Readers*, which were full of weird facts.

So I didn't explain. I just shrugged. 'I like trivia.'

Farley's eyes got even wider behind his glasses. 'You're coming with me,' he said. Then he grabbed my arm and started pulling me down the hall.

'Where are we going?'

'We need one more member. You're exactly what we're missing.'

'Member for what?'

But he didn't answer. He just took me up the stairs to a classroom on the third floor and pulled me inside.

Six other kids were already in there, eating lunch. They'd pushed eight desks together in the middle of the room so they faced each other – two rows of four. On the desks sat a black box with red buttons on top. It looked like something out of a low-budget sci-fi movie.

'Hey, everyone,' Farley said, out of breath by now, 'this is Henry. He's joining our team.'

'*What* team?' I said.

'Reach For The Top. It's kind of like *Jeopardy!* for kids, except you compete against teams instead of individuals.'

Meaning, it's the kind of team that attracts nerds the way dog poop attracts flies.

Before June 1st, this would have been a dream come true. I love this kind of stuff. But I saw what happened to Jesse in high school. High school can be a game-changer.

When you're little, you can let your freak flag fly. You can tell people all the weird things you know. You can sing in public. You can go to the park wearing tighty-whities over your pants and pretend you're the Great Dane or another one of your favorite wrestlers from the Global Wrestling Federation. I know this because Jesse and I used to do it all the time.

But when you get older, all that changes. You learn

that it's best to fly under the radar. I know I can't change my stupid red hair or my stupid freckles. But I *can* lower my freak flag.

So I tried to say thanks but no thanks, but before I could get the words out, Farley was introducing me to the other kids. 'Henry, meet Parvana, Shen, Ambrose, Jerome, Koula, and Alberta.' They all smiled and said hi.

Except for Alberta.

Her head stayed buried in a copy of *Us Weekly*. I recognized her; we're in Home Ec together. I even spoke to her once. We were sitting across from each other at our sewing stations last week, and I said, 'Why are you called Alberta? Why not Saskatchewan, or Manitoba?'

And she said, 'Wow, new guy. Original. Never heard that one before.'

Rude.

You know that song they used to sing on *Sesame Street* – 'One of These Things is Not Like the Others'? Alberta is that thing. Aside from her, everyone in that room *looked* like they belonged on a Reach For The Top team.

Consider these facts:

The boy named Ambrose wore a ratty-looking multi-colored toque, with a pom-pom on top. Indoors. He also wore neon-green socks.

The one named Shen clutched a RUBIK'S CUBE. Need I say more.

Parvana wore a T-shirt that read *The Geek Shall Inherit the Earth*.

Koula snorted. I don't mean once or twice; I mean, all the time. Quiet little snorts, every few seconds. Like a nervous tic.

Jerome wore sweatpants and a shirt that rode up his stomach to reveal layers of flabby white flesh, *and he didn't even seem to care*. Yeah, yeah, I'm one to talk, but if I'm twenty pounds overweight, Jerome is at least a hundred. And I would never, *ever* let my wobblies show!!

Now consider Alberta.

Her hair is short, brown, and spiky – a lot like the Great Dane's, just a different color. She has a gold stud in her nose and one above her eyebrow. Some people might call her chubby, but as someone who has been called that once or twice myself, I prefer the term 'well proportioned.' She was wearing a plaid skirt with a big gold safety pin that stopped just above her knees, black tights, and purple Doc Martens. On top she wore a white T-shirt with the slogan *John Deere Tractors*.

She is the opposite of nerd.

Then my Socials teacher, Mr Jankovich, came into the room. He's a grown-up nerd. All you have to do is look at his feet: he wears Birkenstocks with white tube socks. Even in winter!

'Coach, this is Henry,' Farley told him. 'He's going to join the team.'

No, I'm not, I wanted to say, but Mr Jankovich didn't give me a chance. 'Hey, Henry. That's great news. Everyone, take a seat.'

I was officially trapped. I wanted to kill Farley, and I think he knew it because, even though he sat right across from me, he wouldn't meet my gaze.

Mr Jankovich gave us each a cord, which we inserted into the black box. Each cord had a red button on the end. If you pressed it, it buzzed, and one of eight red lights on top of the box lit up.

Jerome, Koula, Shen, and I sat facing Ambrose, Parvana, Farley, and Alberta.

Mr Jankovich started firing questions at us. They were broken into different categories, like Open Questions, Team Questions, Snap-starts, and Who Am I's. Here are the questions I remember:

1) *In the Internet world, what does URL stand for?* (I had no idea. But Shen and Farley knew: Uniform Resource Locator.)
2) *What river did Julius Caesar cross?* (The Rubicon. I knew that.)
3) *In 55 BCE*, what island did Caesar and his legions invade? (No clue. But Parvana knew it was Britain.)

19

4) *On the periodic table of elements, what does Cd stand for?* (Cadmium. I would have guessed that if Shen hadn't buzzed in first.)

5) *Spelling round. How do you spell beguiled, utopian, incessant, dichotomy?* (I got *utopian* right, and Ambrose buzzed in first on the other three.)

6) *How many baby teeth do humans have? How many adult teeth?* (Twenty and thirty-two. Answered by yours truly.)

7) *Which Hollywood actor is related to José Ferrer, Rosemary Clooney, and Debby Boone?* (George Clooney. Alberta got that one right. She only buzzed in for questions about movie stars and pop music.)

I confess: the lunch hour flew by. As Farley and I walked back to our lockers, he said, 'Next practice is on Tuesday. Be there or be trapezoid.'

'Huh?'

'Square.'

'I'm not joining the team,' I said.

'Oh, you'll join,' he said as we arrived at our lockers.

'What makes you so sure?'

As if on cue, Alberta appeared from around a corner, clutching a binder that was covered in doodles.

'Hi,' I said.

She just scowled and kept walking.

Rude.

Farley smirked. '*That's* what makes me so sure.'

I could feel my face turn red, which, when you already have red hair and freckles, is *not* a good look. 'Her? Please. She's a total stuck-up.'

But Farley grinned smugly as he closed his locker door. 'See you in gym class,' he said. Then he walked off down the hall, listing sideways, humming to himself.

Saturday, January 26

INTRIGUING FACT: Post-traumatic stress disorder (or PTSD) is a severe anxiety disorder that can happen after exposure to a horrifying event.

Or so says Cecil. He talked a lot about PTSD at our session after school yesterday. Which made me talk to him in Robot-Voice. Which made him change tactics.

'You writing in your journal at all?' he asked.

'No,' I lied.

'Oh. Sorry to hear that.'

'I'm not.'

He stared at me for what felt like a whole minute. I stared right back. 'Tell me about your T-shirt,' he finally said. 'Who's the guy?'

'It's the Great Dane.'

Cecil looked at me blankly.

'From the GWF.'

Another blank look.

'The Global Wrestling Federation? *Saturday Night Smash-Up, Monday Night Meltdown?*' Inside I was thinking, *Holy Moly, do you live under a rock?*

'Oh. I've heard of them. I don't own a TV,' he said. A little smugly, if you ask me.

'*Saturday Night Smash-Up* is my favorite show,' I told him. In fact, it was my entire family's favorite show. Mom would make a huge bowl of popcorn, and we'd all gather round the TV every Saturday night, even in the months leading up to IT. We all had a favorite wrestler: Mom's was El Toro; Dad's was the Twister. Jesse's was the same as mine.

'Tell me about the Great Dane,' Cecil said.

'He weighs 198 pounds. That sounds like a lot, but in the GWF, he's a pip-squeak. He wears tight red trunks with white trim and white lace-up boots, and he has short spiked blond hair. His upper body is straight out of Popeye. His signature move is the Body Splash.'

'The Body Splash?'

I did my best to describe it to Cecil. 'Say his opponent is sprawled on the mat. The Great Dane climbs the ropes that surround the ring. He crouches down low . . .' For this part, I stood up on my chair to demonstrate. 'Then he *leaps* into the air. For a moment, it looks like he's flying. Then he lands, stomach-first, across his opponent's chest. *THWACK!*'

I got down on my stomach on his tiny office floor for effect. It was disgusting down there – armies of dust bunnies and a carpet encrusted with bits of old food. 'Imagine the letter *t*,' I said, standing up quickly and brushing myself off. 'That's what it would look like from above.'

'Holy Moly,' said Cecil. 'Sounds violent.'

I rolled my eyes. 'It's more than that. There are story

23

lines and everything. It's super-exciting. High stakes. Good versus evil.'

'Why is the Great Dane your favorite?'

'Because,' I said, a little impatient. 'He's one of the good guys. He's a babyface. And he always has to fight the heels – these huge, butt-ugly bad guys.'

'Does he win?'

'Once in a while. Mostly he loses.'

'So he's an underdog.'

'Yeah.'

For some reason, Cecil started nodding a lot, like we were having a meaningful conversation.

'You never know what's going to happen next,' I continued. 'Wrestlers who've been heels for years become babyfaces, and vice versa. Just when you think you've got someone pegged, he switches sides.'

'So, nobody is one hundred per cent good or evil,' he said. 'Just like real life.'

'Exactly! I bet Stalin opened a door for an old lady once, or hugged his mom. And maybe Mother Teresa spanked a kid, or stole a chocolate bar.'

'I bet the Great Dane was Jesse's favorite, too. Am I right?'

Suddenly I had goose bumps. How had he figured that out? It gave me the creeps. 'I plead the Fifth,' I said.

'Do you even know what that means?'

'I saw it on a TV show. It means *I'm not answering the question and you can't make me.*'

Cecil smiled. 'OK. Session's almost over, anyway.' He stood up and pumped my hand. 'I think we made good progress today, Henry.'

I was like, *What? All we talked about was wrestling!!*

I don't mind Cecil. He seems like an OK guy. But there's a joke my dad told me once that describes Cecil perfectly: 'What do you call a guy who gets fifty-one per cent in medical school? *Doctor.*'

11:00 p.m.

We had take-out pizza again for dinner. I forced myself to eat only four slices.

Dad drank only one beer with his Rapiflux pill. He started taking Rapiflux about four months ago. I thought it was to help with indigestion or something, till I looked it up on Dad's laptop. Rapiflux is another brand name for Fluoxetine. Which is another word for Prozac. Which, according to the website, 'increases one's sense of well-being, counteracting tendencies to depression.'

We were eating our pizza in front of the TV when the phone rang. We don't have call display cos it's extra, but I knew who it was.

'Hello?'

'Hi, Henry.'

Yup. Mom.

'How's my Smaller Fry?' She's called me that my whole life. Jesse was Small Fry. I guess if she'd had a third kid, he would have been Smallest Fry.

'Good.'

'How's the new school?' She asks me this every time.

'Fine.'

'Let me guess – your favorite class is English?'

'Yes.'

'You've always had a way with words.'

There was a long silence after this, which my English teacher, Mr Schell, would say was a fine example of irony.

'How's Dad?'

I looked over at Dad, who was gazing at a spot somewhere east of the TV. 'Good,' I said. *Saturday Night Smash-Up* is about to start.'

This was followed by another long pause, then she said, 'I'm sorry, Henry.' And just like all the other phone calls, she started to cry. And just like all the other phone calls, I passed the phone to my dad because I am tired of her tears.

Dad took the phone into his bedroom and closed the door. I listened to the rise and fall of their voices. Sometimes Dad shouts on these calls, but tonight he talked quietly, and after twenty minutes or so, he joined me back on the couch. He gave me a big smile. It was the phoniest smile ever, but I appreciated the effort. 'So what'd I miss?'

I told him that the Great Dane had lost his match against Vlad the Impaler, who'd brought him down with a Bionic Elbow (which means he smashed his elbow on top of the Great Dane's head). Vlad also gave the Dane the old Testicular Claw, which is pretty much what it sounds like. It's illegal, but Vlad waited till the ref turned away, so he didn't get caught.

Now Dad's in his room, and I'm in mine. In the ad on Craigslist, the apartment was advertised as *one bdrm den*. I am in the *den*. I think *den* was a misprint and the owner really meant to write *closet*.

Our building is a four-storey gray stucco box from the 1960s that sits right on Broadway, the busiest street in Kitsilano. It's called the Cedar Manor, a fancy name that is *so* not deserved. In fact, if I were to describe the Manor in one word, that word would be 'ugly.' The orange, green, and brown carpeting in the corridors looks like it hasn't been cleaned since the place was built. The walls are grimy. The lights are fluorescent and they hum.

But I'm not complaining. Vancouver is a way more expensive city to live in than Port Salish, and with Dad not having his own business anymore and Mom not working and the Marlin family launching a lawsuit, I figure I'm lucky we're not living in a pup tent in Stanley Park.

Besides, here in Vancouver we are completely anonymous. In Port Salish, everyone knew everyone. I liked that, growing up. But after IT happened, it was a curse.

Still, I'd be lying if I said I didn't miss our house. It was a real honest-to-goodness home, with a yard and everything. It wasn't fancy, but Jesse and I had our own bedrooms, which was good because Jesse was a pig. I, on the other hand, am neat and tidy. 'Bordering on anal retentive,' I once heard my mom tell my dad, when she didn't know I was listening.

So what if I like everything in its proper place? My room here is half the size of my room in Port Salish, but my poster of the Great Dane is still perfectly centered over my bed, which I make every morning with hospital corners. I have a portable shelving unit in my closet, where I fold my socks and underwear. Everything else – jeans, sweatshirts, T-shirts, mostly in shades of blue or gray – is on hangers. I can't stand a wrinkly T-shirt. You could say I'm obsessed with a neat if nondescript appearance and personal hygiene in general. Some people think that if you're fat, you're also dirty, but that is false. Just because I have wobblies doesn't mean I don't shower and use a high-powered deodorant.

Near the end, it was obvious that Jesse wasn't using deodorant. Or showering. Or changing his clothes as often as he should. He tried to mask his b.o. with AXE bodyspray, which only made it worse.

We barely talked to each other in the six months leading up to IT, and when we did, it wasn't very nice.

'Quit stinking up the can, Meatloaf,' he'd say to me most mornings because a) my system is like clockwork, and I always have a dump first thing in the morning, and b) I was already a little bit on the chubby side.

'Bite me, Pizza Face,' I'd retort. Then I'd catch a whiff of his b.o. '*Ew*, you think my *poo* reeks?? *You* reek!'

'Small Fry, why don't you have a quick shower?' my mom would say when we joined her in the kitchen. 'It'll take you five minutes. I'll make you some cinnamon toast for when you get out.'

'I don't want any f---ing cinnamon toast. Leave me the f--- alone.' Jesse swore a lot during those last six months.

Then he'd storm out of the room, and my mom would try not to cry.

He never used to talk to her like that. To me, sure, but that's what brothers do. He and Mom, though, they were tight. Bonded. Like Super Glue.

I couldn't help but envy them in a fairly big way. I wanted what they had, but I also knew I never could, because Jesse was her firstborn. They'd had two whole years to fall in love with each other before I came along.

I saw this movie once, when I was home with a fever. It was on some cable channel, and I have no idea why I watched it because it was seriously old, but I guess I was

29

so feverish I couldn't even lift the remote. Anyway, it was called *Ordinary People*, and it was about a family with two sons. The boys had been in a boating accident, and the older one drowned and the younger one survived. The mom was so mean to her younger son! And she finally admitted that she wished he'd died, instead.

I'm not saying that my mom has had the same thought. But it's just another thing that knocks around in my head sometimes, when I picture her in a loony bin on the other side of the country, far away from us.

It's something I think about when sleep won't come.

1:00 a.m.
Speaking of sleep. It is highly overrated. Sleep + IT = Nightmares. Blood. Gore. ~~Plastic yellow tube slides~~.

2:00 a.m.
What's-his-head from next door, Mr Atapattu, is watching the Home Shopping Network again. I can hear it through the wall. 'Order your Slap-Happy today!'

What a freak.

Tuesday, January 29

INTRIGUING FACT: In 1929, this man named Noah John Rondeau decided he'd had enough of people, so he became a hermit. He lived alone in the Adirondack Mountains and called himself Mayor of Cold River City, Population: 1.

Before IT happened, I would have said this guy was a weirdo. But now I get it. It's not that I suddenly don't like people; it's just that I can't engage with them *all the time*. These days, a little bit goes a long way, if that makes any sense. Dad usually doesn't get back from his construction jobs till after six, and that suits me just fine. After a full day of classes and teachers and now Farley, I need some quality hermit time when I get home.

But try telling that to the Vultures.

Vulture 1: Karen Vargas – Apt. 311

Dad and I had barely started carrying stuff from our U-Haul up to our apartment three weeks ago, when Karen stepped out of the building and marched right up to our truck. She was wearing a short skirt and a top that showed off way too much flesh in the boobular area. Her shoes were what my mom would call highly impractical. I think she thought she looked youthful, but she didn't; she must be as old as my mom.

She held a paper plate full of cookies.

'Howdy, neighbors,' she said as she handed my dad the plate. 'Just a little housewarming treat. Baked them myself last night.'

My dad just looked at her like he was in a drug-induced stupor, which, come to think of it, he was.

'Oh. Thanks,' he said.

'My name's Karen. Karen Vargas.' She waited for my dad to tell her his name, but since IT happened, Dad often forgets basic social skills.

'And your name is?' she finally asked.

'Pete. Pete Larsen. This is my son, Henry.'

'Nice to meet you, Pete. And Henry,' she added, not even looking at me. 'You guys must be moving into 211?'

My dad nodded.

'I'm directly upstairs from you. 311. Did you know the last tenant in your place was running a meth lab?'

That roused my dad a little bit. I know I perked up.

'Seriously?' I asked, even though she still didn't look at me.

'Didn't the landlord tell you? No, why would he? Probably thought it would scare you away. The guy who lived there was cooking crystal meth. We only found out cos he started a fire one day. The whole building could've blown up with all of us inside!'

'Wow.' That's my dad these days: man of few words.

'I always knew there was something sinister about that guy,' she said, which I didn't believe for a second. After my brother did what he did, people who barely knew him were quoted in the paper saying things like, 'I always felt uneasy around that kid,' or, 'He scared me.' Which was a huge steaming pile of bull turds. Jesse never scared anyone.

'If you boys ever need anything, you know where to find me,' she said with a smile, and I thought, *How does she know it's just us boys? How does she know my mom isn't going to step out the front door at any moment?* I think she must've asked the superintendent who was moving in.

Anyway, Dad just gave Karen a vague half-smile, then the two of us headed into the building, carrying our enormous coffee table. He didn't thank her for the cookies or anything, just left her shivering on the sidewalk. Which was fine by me. Later that evening, after we'd finished unloading the truck, I unwrapped the cookies. They were so obviously store-bought. Chips Ahoy! is my best guess.

Still, I ate them all in one sitting. Which didn't help with my wobblies. Not one bit.

Vulture 2: Mr Atapattu – Apt. 213

Mr Atapattu knocked on our door while we were unpacking.

'Hello,' he said when I answered. 'I am your next-door neighbor, in 213.' He smiled, revealing a mouth full of crooked yellow teeth. He was dressed neatly in a cardigan and beige pants. I'm guessing he's in his sixties, but I honestly have no idea. Everyone over thirty just looks old to me.

'I brought you a housewarming treat. Homemade coconut *barfi*.' He held out a plate.

'Barfy?' I repeated.

'It's an Indian sweet,' he said. 'I'm Sri Lankan, but I cook foods from many regions.'

I took the plate to be polite, then my dad came to the door, and he and Mr Atapattu shook hands. 'I just thought I should introduce myself,' Mr Atapattu continued, with an accent that made each word sound dignified. 'It's important to know your neighbors. You probably heard about the man who lived here before you. Not a good man. I complained that I smelled chemicals, but Yuri, the superintendent, didn't believe me. He thought I was engaged in a 'tit for tat' because a few of the tenants had complained about my cooking smells.'

'Oh,' my dad replied. Yup, he's a real conversationalist these days.

There was an awkward silence after that. It dawned on me that Mr Atapattu was hoping we'd invite him in. 'If you need any assistance . . .'

'No, we're good. But thanks,' said my dad. Mr Atapattu's smile quivered slightly as my dad walked away from the door. I wanted to tell him not to take it personally, that lately my dad is more like a hologram of himself – there, but not there.

Instead, I said, 'Thanks for the barf.'

'Barfi.'

Then I closed the door.

The *barfi* was delicious. Way better than Karen's 'home-made' cookies. I ate all the *barfi* in one sitting, too.

Still. I don't want food from them. I don't want anything from them, except for them to leave us alone.

But they don't. When I got home today, Karen was at her mailbox. She was wearing tight jeans and another pair of highly impractical shoes.

'Hey, Harry,' she said with a smile.

'Henry.'

'You and your dad settling in OK?'

I nodded as I opened our mailbox.

'So it's just the two of you, huh?'

'My mom will be joining us any day now,' I replied.

Her smile vanished. 'Oh. Where is she?' she said as she dumped her junk mail onto the ledge in front of the mailboxes.

I wanted to say, *None of your damn business*, but instead I said, 'She travels a lot. For work.' Which was a big fat lie, but whatever.

When I finally escaped Vulture 1, Vulture 2 pounced.

Mr Atapattu poked his head out just as I was unlocking our door. I swear he stands there, staring through the peep-hole, waiting for someone to walk past. 'Good day, Henry.'

'Hi, Mr Atapattu.'

'Forgive me, but do you have the plate I gave you last week?'

'Oh. Yeah.' I went inside and found the plate, stacked amongst a pile of our own dishes, and handed it to him.

'Thank you,' I said. 'The *barfi* was really good.'

Mr Atapattu beamed. 'Would you like to come in? I could make us some tea.' He must have seen the look on my face because he said, 'Oh, of course. Stranger danger. Wait one moment, then.' He disappeared into his apart-ment. A minute later, he returned with a plastic container full of what looked like a thick yellow soup.

'It's a vegetable curry.' He handed it to me. 'I see your dad through my living-room window, coming home with a pizza every night . . .' He said it almost apologetically, which I thought was appropriate since he was admitting that he spied on us. 'A growing boy needs his vegetables.' I swear he glanced at my wobblies when he said that.

'Thanks,' I said. 'Oh, is that our phone?' It wasn't, but it gave me an excuse to hurry back to our apartment and lock the door.

When Dad came home – with a bucket of KFC, not pizza, so there – we ate the vegetable curry as a side dish.

The first few bites weren't bad. Then my nose started running, and my tongue started to burn, and I had to stop. I ate seven pieces of chicken and a pile of fries instead.

'That chicken was supposed to last us two nights, Henry,' my dad said when he looked into the empty bucket.

I just belched.

I'm thinking I might have to start using the back entrance to avoid the Vultures. As my mom says, 'Certain people, if you give them an inch, they'll take a mile.'

Karen and Mr Atapattu *are* those people. Their loneliness is like a bad egg fart – you can smell it a mile away.

Dad and I, we have a different kind of loneliness. It's the kind you feel, even when you're with someone else, because you know something, or someone, is missing.

Other lonely people can't fill that emptiness.

Other lonely people only remind you how alone you already are.

Other lonely people only make it worse.

Friday, February 1

I managed to avoid Farley and the Reach For The Top practice on Tuesday by hiding out in a study carrel in the library. But today, I wasn't so lucky. We had gym together before lunch, and when it was over, Farley followed me out of the change room.

'C'mon, the team really needs you,' Farley said for the fiftieth time as we got our lunches out of our lockers. 'Please, please, pretty please.'

'Fine,' I said. 'But I have to pee. I'll meet you there.' This was a lie. Not the *pee* part – the other part.

But when I came out of the washroom, Farley was standing right outside the door, bouncing up and down on his heels.

'Let's go.' He grabbed my hand, just as Troy and his friends walked past.

Honestly, Farley's timing sucks.

Troy made loud kissing sounds. 'Aw, what a cute couple!' he said. 'Fatty and Skinny!' Then he grabbed Farley's nipple through his shirt and twisted it, hard. 'Purple nurple,' he said as he walked away.

I wanted to give Troy a Body Splash, followed by a Testicular Claw.

'*Ow*,' Farley murmured, letting go of my hand to rub

his chest. 'C'mon, we're going to be late.' Then he tried to grab my hand again.

I shook my hand free. 'No! I'm not going.'

Farley looked kind of hurt, but so what? 'Fine,' he said. 'Your loss. If you change your mind, it's room 341.'

Then he walked away, tilting to the left.

I went to the cafeteria, but it was packed and I didn't know anyone. So I headed to the library and sat at a study carrel far away from the librarian, who'd posted a big NO FOOD OR DRINK sign at the entrance. I pulled out my lunch – day-old pizza and two bags of chips that Dad buys in bulk from the Superstore.

The librarian must have a bloodhound's sense of smell because she swooped down on me before I'd taken one bite. 'Can't you read?' she hissed.

So I packed up my stuff and went outside. It was drizzling, and the stoners had already taken shelter under the closest tree.

Suddenly, out of nowhere, a wave of homesickness washed over me. In Port Salish, I never, ever had to eat lunch alone. Me and Jodie would always eat together, and a whole bunch of other kids would eat with us, too. It was just the way it was at our elementary school. It hadn't dawned on us yet to divvy up into stupid little cliques.

In Port Salish, my mom made our lunches every day,

before she left for work. A sandwich on whole wheat bread, even though we begged for white. Homemade cookies. A Baggie with mini-carrots or some other vegetable or fruit. A juice box. She made sure we ate pretty healthy. She made sure I didn't get wobblies.

Sometimes we'd find little notes tucked into our lunch bags. Like if I had Math, she might write *Mmm, I love pi!* Or if Jesse had Science, she might write *Why do chemists like nitrates so much? Because they're cheaper than day rates!* Once in a while, Dad would toss in a note too, like *Ask Mr Tomlinson where he bought his hairpiece*, or, *Remember to count Mrs Stanley's nose hairs today.*

And then I started thinking about how often I'd complained about Mom's lunches, and I felt furious with myself because what I wouldn't give to have her making my lunches again. So I bolted away from stupid Trafalgar Secondary and walked the ten blocks to my stupid new apartment. I could feel my jeans cutting into my stupid wobblies, and I was hating myself so much that I didn't see stupid Mr Atapattu in the lobby until it was too late.

'Hi, Henry,' he said, smiling and showing off his crooked yellow teeth. He must've seen my expression because he added, 'Is everything OK?'

I couldn't even pretend to be polite. I just walked past him and took the stairs two at a time to our apartment because I didn't want to wait for the elevator. I ate my crap lunch while I watched crap daytime TV, and I had a third bag of chips, even though I and my wobblies knew I shouldn't.

When I was done with my lunch, I snuck into Dad's bedroom and pulled the shoebox out from under his bed.

'Dickhead,' I whispered.

Then I went into my own room and crawled into bed.

I'm still in bed.

I'll stay here till Dad comes home.

4:15 p.m.

The phone's ringing. It's probably Cecil. I'm supposed to be sitting in his crappy little office at the health center right now.

4:30 p.m.

The phone is ringing *again*. Third time in a row. Cecil may not be a good therapist, but I give him marks for persistence.

5:00 p.m.

When I was in the boys' washroom today, I noticed someone had written *School is Hell* on one of the stall doors.

I pulled out my own pen, put an *X* through the word *School*, and wrote *Life*.

Saturday, February 2

3:00 a.m.

I dreamed about my brother again. Not about IT, but about the Other Thing. I could hear Jesse screaming. I tried to run toward him, but it was like I was running through pea soup. Then I heard the sound of duct tape being pulled off a roll.

Dad woke me up. He said I was yelling in my sleep.

4:00 a.m.

Now Dad and I are both in the living room, watching TV. I'm in my pjs and Dad's wearing the robe Mom made him a zillion Christmases ago. It's made of navy blue velour, with a patch on the chest that says *World's Greatest Dad*.

It's a strange TV landscape at 4:00 a.m. on a Saturday morning. Among the infomercials, we've found an old black-and-white movie called *Bringing up Baby*. The baby is a leopard. Seriously. It stars some famous dead actors. Their lines are fast and funny, but I still feel a bit anxious that one of them might get mauled to death by the leopard at any moment. It doesn't seem like that kind of movie, but sometimes you can be in for a rude surprise.

6:00 a.m.

Phew. Nobody was mauled. I liked that movie.

Wouldn't it be amazing if you could write the movie

script for your own life? I guess it would have lots of boring bits. But at least you could write yourself a happy ending.

Later

After Dad and I got up for real at around eleven, we went shopping for supplies for our earthquake kit. We already have a lot of items, like sleeping bags and flashlights and a good first-aid kit, because of all the camping we've done. But today we were after food. We drove to an outdoor store called the Three Vets and stocked up on Meals-Ready-to-Eat (MREs as they're called in the military). You can just cut open the bag and squeeze the food right into your mouth if you want. Dad and I tried a bag of corned beef hash when we got home, and it wasn't half-bad.

'We'll keep the kit in the hall closet,' Dad said as he put the MREs into a huge plastic bin along with our other supplies. 'They say you should keep it near the front door so you can grab it on your way out.'

I didn't have the heart to tell him that if we do have an earthquake, we'll have bigger things to worry about than trying to grab our kit, like the third and fourth floors collapsing on top of us.

Dad has been obsessed with building this kit from the moment we moved here. Don't get me wrong: we *should* have an earthquake kit, living in BC. But we never had a kit in Port Salish. My parents never got around to it.

I don't need a degree in psychology to know what Cecil would say: *Your father couldn't stop the first disaster, so now he's trying to plan ahead for the next disaster so the outcome won't be as devastating.*

See, Dad thinks the first disaster was his fault.

It was his gun.

Dad owned an old hunting rifle that had belonged to my grandpa Kaspar Larsen, who died before I was born. (That is what the *K* stands for in my name, but I don't advertise it.) Once a year, during deer season, Dad would go hunting with a few of his buddies. He must have shot a few deer because I remember eating venison once in a while.

He was very careful with the gun. It was locked away in a special cabinet. He followed all the safety instructions. But Jesse must've figured out where he kept the key. And on June 1st, Jesse got the key and opened the cabinet and took out the rifle before the rest of us woke up. He also knew where Dad kept the bullets. He loaded the rifle – we found out later he'd visited a website to learn how – and placed it in his gym bag. He left while we were still sleeping. We found a note on the kitchen table: *Gone to school early. I'm sorry. Love you. Jesse.*

The *sorry* part was weird. The *love you* part was even weirder.

When he got to school, he carried the gym bag with

him to his first class. How do I know this? I know because I can read, and the papers interviewed anyone and everyone who'd seen my brother that day. They all said he acted the same as always, which meant he didn't talk to anyone. He kept to himself.

Except he carried the gym bag with him, and he didn't even have gym that day.

Just before second period, Jesse saw Scott Marlin at his locker. He put the bag on the floor and took out the rifle.

'Hey, Scott,' he said.

If Scott had known what was coming, he might have chosen his words more carefully for once in his life. But he didn't. 'Did I say you could speak to me, Ballsack?'

While all of this was unfolding at the high school, I was right down the block at the elementary school. We'd just finished gym, where we were square-dancing with the girls. I had 'do-si-doed' with Jodie. The bell rang for lunch, and we were all about to head outside when the principal's voice came on the speaker system. She told us we were forbidden to leave the school; we were in lockdown.

We were sent back to our classrooms. At first, it was kind of fun; we were all trying to guess what might be happening outside. Jason thought it was a drug bust nearby. Emily thought it might be a terrorist attack. Then Anna checked her phone.

You weren't allowed to use any electronic devices during lockdown, but Anna did anyway. Suddenly she said, 'There's been a shooting at the high school.' That was all the information she had, found on a local news website. Our teacher yelled at her, then took away her phone.

And it wasn't kind of fun anymore. A lot of us had brothers and sisters at the high school. We had no idea what was going on, or how bad it was. Jodie started to cry. I held her hand.

I know what she was thinking, because I was thinking it, too: *What if my brother is hurt?* I never – not once – imagined that my brother was the shooter.

About an hour later, our principal came to the classroom door; some police officers stood behind her. 'Jodie Marlin and Henry Larsen, can you come with me, please?' Her voice was shaking.

Jodie started to cry again. I was numb. When we got outside, one officer directed Jodie to her car; another officer directed me to his. 'Can we go together?' I asked. The cop shook his head.

When we got to the station, I was brought into a room where my parents sat. I didn't need to be a genius to know something awful had happened; but it still didn't occur to me that my brother was behind it. When they told me, I didn't believe it. Then I was whisked out of the room so the police could give Mom and Dad the grisly details.

My parents tried to shield me from the worst of it. But all you have to do is a Google search and a whole pile of articles pop up. I couldn't stop myself. Whenever they were out of the house, which was a lot in those first couple of weeks, I read everything I could find. That's how I found out that after Jesse shot Scott in the chest, Scott's friends tried their best to stop the bleeding. It's also how I found out that my brother's body was discovered under the stairwell a minute later. He'd shot himself in the head.

I learned other things I hadn't known before, like that Scott had wanted to join the Canadian Armed Forces after high school. Many articles said he was devoted to his two younger sisters, but I already knew that because one of his sisters was my best friend, Jodie.

I just had a chest pain. Can you have a heart attack when you're thirteen?

Anyway. I respected the local reporter because he also dug up a lot of stuff about the constant bullying my brother had put up with, including some incidents my parents and I had never heard about: The 'Jesse Larsen's a Faggot' fan page on Facebook that quickly got shut down, but not before Jesse saw it – and the fifty-two 'fans' it had acquired in less than a week; the 'accidental' tripping in the hallway that sent him to the hospital for stitches (we knew about the stitches, of course, but not that Scott had sent him head-first into the water fountain); the dog poop Jesse found in his locker one day. That reporter looked at the story from all sides. But a lot of other articles I read were peppered with lies. Some so-called 'experts', people who didn't even know us, suggested that my parents must have been abusive, or absent, or stupid.

These people were wrong. From the beginning of high school, my parents worried about Jesse all the time. They talked to the guidance counselor and to our family doctor a million times. Mom even took Jesse to a therapist once, but Jesse didn't like her and refused to go back. Mom had him on a waiting list for another one, but then IT happened, and the appointment was no longer necessary.

The lies that hurt the most were the ones that were told by people we knew. One of our neighbors, an old lady named Alice Clayburn, told a reporter that she'd seen us performing witchcraft in our backyard. I wracked my brain over that one. All I could come up with was that once, about three years ago, I'd found a wounded kingfisher with Jodie, and we'd carried it back to my house in an old towel. Jesse and I kept it in the yard and tried to feed it, but it died the next day. So we buried it in the yard while Jesse pretended to be a minister, saying stuff like, 'We commit his body to the ground,' which he'd heard on a TV show.

Witchcraft, my butt. And to think that Jesse had mowed that old bag's lawn two summers in a row. For free!!

Gord Saunders, one of Jesse's classmates, told a national newspaper that when Jesse was ten, he used to torture cats for fun.

LIE!!!! And the paper printed it!!!! I wanted to find Gord *and* the reporter after that and give them both the Testicular Claw.

It was like Jesse was one person when he was alive and another after he died. When he was alive, Jesse was the babyface. Scott was the heel. But the day Jesse took Dad's rifle to school, they switched roles. Scott became the babyface, and Jesse became the heel.

Oh, man. I suddenly get why Cecil seemed so pleased in our last session. I'd been talking about wrestling; he'd been talking about my brother.

One big glaring difference, Cecil.

On *Saturday Night Smash-Up*, everyone comes out of it alive.

Monday, February 4

INTRIGUING FACT: The most poisonous animals on earth are often the most colorful. Why? Because they *want* to be seen. That way predators have to eat only a couple of them before their buddies go, 'Hang on. If I eat this colorful dart frog/coral snake/monarch butterfly, I'm going to die a very painful death, just like my buddy Bob!' Pretty soon everyone knows to leave them alone.

Alberta is a human version of the dart frog. You can't help but notice her; but you learn very quickly that she's toxic.

Like today in Home Ec. I sat at the sewing machine facing hers. Alberta was wearing a cut-off jean skirt with green-and-white striped tights underneath and a powder blue T-shirt with a picture of a tabby cat in a sweater, playing the piano. On her head was a red beret.

'OK, class,' said Mrs Bardus, 'today we're going to use the sewing machine to finish our tote bags.' For the past few classes, we've been cutting out fabric and using fabric paint to create designs. I painted a bunch of tulips. Alberta painted a skull and crossbones.

As per usual, she acted like I wasn't even there, but then her thread got tangled up in the bobbin. 'Hey, new guy,' she said. 'Help.'

No 'please,' no nothing. But my mother raised me to

be a gentleman. I got up and moved around to her station. She didn't even budge over an inch or anything, which meant that as I was showing her how to rethread her machine, I was forced to breathe in the scent of her hair. (It smelled like tropical fruits. But still.)

I sat back down. 'Next time, you'll be able to do it yourself,' I told her. 'And the name's Henry.'

She didn't answer. Not even a thank you.

Rude.

A good five minutes later, she said, 'Where did you learn to sew?' It took me a moment to realize she was talking to *me*.

'My mom taught me the basics a couple of years ago. So I could make my own Halloween costume.'

'What was the costume?'

My ears prickled, and I was pretty sure they were turning pink. 'Captain Underpants.'

She laughed. '*Ha-ha-ha-ha-ha-ha-HEEE-haw*.' It was like machine-gun fire, followed by a donkey's bray. 'What was it, a giant pair of Y-fronts?'

'Better than that,' I said. 'It was a flesh-colored one-piece. With buttons for the nipples and belly button. I stuffed it full of pillows, then we bought an enormous pair of underwear to put over top.'

'Awesome,' she said, and I actually think she meant it. 'Who are you going to give your tote bag to?'

'My mom.'

'I'm going to give mine to my older sister,' she said. 'Cos it's ugly, like her.' Then she smiled and looked right at me, and it was the first time I noticed she had a lazy eye.

'What's your sister's name?' I asked.

'Ontario.'

'Seriously?'

'No. Her name's Cricket.'

'Stop.'

'I poop you not. Mom got to choose her name, and her favorite soap-opera character on *The Young and the Restless* was called Cricket.' She sighed. 'Yup. We are total white trash.'

'Who picked your name?'

'My dad. They were living in Fort McMurray, Alberta, when I was – you know – *conceived*.' She pretended to gag.

'Look on the bright side. At least they didn't call you Fort McMurray. And at least you weren't conceived in Newfoundland.'

She laughed again. '*Ha-ha-ha-ha-ha-ha-HEEE-haw!*'

~~It was kind of adorable.~~

In Port Salish, everyone thought I had a crush on Jodie. But they didn't understand that Jodie and I just *got* each other. We both secretly wanted to be contestants on a show called *Are You Smarter Than a 5th Grader?* even though we mocked the show all the time and dubbed it *Are You Smarter Than a Cheese Grater?* We still liked playing with Lego, even though we knew we were too old. And we loved exploring the tide pools together by the ocean's edge at low tide. I still remember the day we found a perfect sand dollar. Perfect! Not a fragment missing, not even a crack. I let Jodie keep it because she'd been having a bad day.

Then my brother did what he did.

I saw Jodie just once after that.

I walked to her house about a week after IT happened. I don't know how I got up the guts to do that. It wasn't bravery, that's for sure. You know when you're having a bad dream and part of you *knows* it's a dream and that part of you is shouting, *It's just a dream! Wake up!* But you don't wake up – you just keep having the nightmare? That's what it felt like as I walked to her house. A part of my brain kept shouting, *Abort mission! Abort mission!* But it was like I was sleepwalking. I just kept going.

Jodie answered the door. She looked terrible. Her face was blotchy and red, and her eyes were puffy from crying. I know I looked just as bad.

We stared at each other, and for a moment I really thought we were going to fall into each other's arms and blubber like a couple of babies.

But then Mr Marlin appeared behind her. His enormous frame filled the doorway. 'What the hell are you doing here?' he shouted, his eyes bulging out of his head. 'Stay away from my family! Stay away from my daughter!'

Then he slammed the door in my face.

After that, I pretty much stayed inside.

I think that's when my wobblies started to grow.

I guess that's when my furies started to grow, too.

I know Jodie's address. Sometimes I think about writing to her, but what would I say? *Seen any good starfish lately? Sorry my brother killed your brother?*

Yeah, no.

Just before dismissal time, Mrs Bardus walked around the room, checking out everyone's sewing. She held up Alberta's and said, 'This is a fine example of shoddy workmanship. However, Henry's here is nicely done.'

Alberta just scowled. Then the bell rang.

'How come you weren't at the Reach For The Top practices last week?' she said as we gathered up our stuff.

I shrugged. 'Farley dragged me there that one time. I never said I was joining.'

Alberta looked at me. Well, one eye looked at me. The other one looked somewhere over my shoulder. 'Let me guess. You think it's too nerdy.'

'Did you see the kids in that room?'

'So? Have you looked in the mirror lately?'

I confess: that hurt. 'Why did *you* join?' I asked her. 'You don't seem—'

'Nerdy enough?'

I was going to say *smart enough*, but I didn't.

'Here's the thing about Reach For The Top,' she said as we walked out of class. 'It's so nerdy, it's crossed back over into cool.'

I snorted.

'Hey, whatevs. If you want to stop yourself from doing something fun cos you're afraid of what other people might think, that is totally your beeswax.' Then she walked away. The green-and-white striped tights only made her big thighs look bigger.

~~They looked spectacular.~~

Dad measured me tonight. I've grown half an inch. Dad said it might just be that I need a haircut because my hair grows up and out instead of down. I told him I didn't appreciate his pessimistic attitude.

A while later, Mom called. I guess I've been really missing her cos I didn't have the energy to do my usual 'one-word answers in a frosty tone' routine. I really wanted to talk to her. 'Did you ever get to watch *Saturday Night Smash-Up?*' I asked. They rerun it on Sunday afternoons, so if she misses it, she can sometimes watch it then.

'No,' she sighed. 'I went to the TV room, but some other patients were already watching a hockey game.'

'Want me to tell you what happened?'

'Please.'

'OK. Close your eyes.' I started with a play-by-play account of the match between El Toro (her favorite) and Jack Knife. It was a great fight. El Toro and Jack Knife used to be best friends, and they'd often partner up in the ring to fight a couple of heels. Then, one day, El Toro got sweet on Jack Knife's ex-girlfriend (another wrestler named Holly Wood), and next time they were in the ring together, Jack Knife turned on El Toro, whacking him in the head with a metal chair. Since then, they have been archenemies.

'It looked like El Toro had it in the bag,' I told her.

'Jack Knife was lying on the mat. El Toro turned away and pumped his fists in the air. So he didn't see Jack Knife stand up. Next thing you know, Jack Knife spins him around and gives him a Bionic Elbow. El Toro dropped like a rag doll.'

'No! Oh, I hate Jack Knife!' she said.

It was a *brilliant* conversation, and no, I'm not being sarcastic. Mom is almost as big a GWF fan as I am, and it's the one thing we can talk about that doesn't end in tears.

Then I made the mistake of telling her about the tote bag, and it ended in tears. 'I wish you were here,' she said.

'Yeah, well,' I replied, my voice frosty again. 'I wish you were *here*.'

From September to December, we'd lived with Pop-Pop and Grams in Picton, Ontario. Growing up, I used to love visiting their place. But not this time. This time, it sucked.

Mom spent a lot of time in bed. She only left the house to see a psychiatrist in Kingston three times a week. Dad picked up a few odd construction jobs through Pop-Pop and Grams's friends. And I went to the local school. But Pop-Pop and Grams had told their closest friends what had happened, and, of course, word spread. So after two weeks of putting up with the stares and whispers of the kids in my class, I announced that I wasn't going back. What's weird is that Mom and Dad didn't even argue with me.

For the next couple of months, I did my work through correspondence school, using Pop-Pop and Grams's ancient PC. I barely left the house. My wobblies grew, and so did my furies.

Just before Christmas, we were sitting at the table eating Grams's meatloaf when Dad said, 'I think we should move to Vancouver.'

My mom dropped her knife and fork. 'What? When?'

'There's a lot of construction work there,' Dad said. 'And I have my license in BC.' He'd co-owned his own construction company in Port Salish, but two months after IT happened, he sold his half to his partner. 'Plus Henry can start at a new school there. Fresh start.'

Mom was quiet.

'What do you think, Henry?' Dad asked, trying to fill the silence.

I liked the idea. A fresh start in a new city, where no one knew our story – it sounded brilliant. Even Pop-Pop and Grams were onboard. They knew we couldn't live with them forever. We decided we'd move after Christmas. Dad lined up the apartment on Craigslist.

But a couple of days before we were supposed to leave, I heard my parents shouting upstairs. Then my mom came down. Her eyes were red. 'Will you go for a walk with me, Henry?'

So even though it was sleeting outside and bitterly cold, I walked with her through the streets of Picton, past the other old redbrick homes and the enormous snow-banks.

'You know how much I love you,' she said, her voice shaking.

I nodded, but I felt sick.

'I'm going to stay with Pop-Pop and Grams for a while longer. Just until I . . .'

The possibilities for the rest of that sentence were endless. *Just until I . . . lose ten pounds on Weight Watchers? Just until I . . . grow a beard? Just until I . . . can start loving you and your dad again?*

Dad tells me all the time that Mom still loves me, but that is very, very hard to believe. Sometimes I feel just as angry at her as I do at Jesse, like if they were standing in front of me right now, I'd give them both a Bionic Elbow.

According to my parents, I used to have terrible temper tantrums when I was little. I can remember lying in the middle of the grocery store aisle, screaming and pounding my fists into the floor because Mom wouldn't buy Cocoa Puffs. I remember that the actual anger didn't last very long; it would switch to humiliation really fast, like somehow I knew, even at three, that I looked like a total dork. That would make me even angrier, only now I'd be angry with myself. My mom always seemed to get it, because she'd scoop me up and hold me really tight against her so I couldn't flail, and eventually I'd get exhausted and go limp in her arms.

But my furies went away, like they do for most kids. Then Jesse did what he did. And every so often, they come back.

The first time it happened was right after Mr Marlin slammed the door in my face, because that's when I really knew it was over for us in Port Salish. People hated me and my family as much as they hated Jesse. So I went home and I tore Jesse's room apart. Then I took his manga collection and ripped every page out of every book.

The second time was the day after Mom said she wasn't going to move to Vancouver with us, and I started speaking in Robot-Voice. I said some really nasty things. 'Mother-bot. You. Are. Totally Pathetic. I Hate. Your Freaking Guts.' 'Go to Hell. Pop-Pop-bot. Do Not. Get Involved.'

That's right. Robot-Henry even swore at his own grandpa.

The day Dad and I caught our plane, Mom didn't even come to the airport. She went to her appointment with her psychiatrist instead. Dr Dumas called us the next day in Vancouver to tell us that Mom was exhibiting signs of a nervous breakdown, so he'd admitted her to the psych ward, where she's been ever since.

I refuse to blame myself.

Jesse made this mess, not me.

After we got off the phone with Mom, Dad and I put on the TV. A few minutes later, someone knocked on our door. I looked through the peephole. It was Mr Atapattu. I think he was holding a plate of food, but I couldn't be sure.

I didn't answer. I just tiptoed back to the couch and tore open a fresh bag of Doritos. Mr Atapattu must've known we were home though, cos the TV was playing quite loud and my dad even called out, 'Who is it, Henry?'

But you know what? Tough.

Wednesday, February 6

So I caved. I went to a Reach For The Top practice at lunch today. Farley was so excited, he did a little dance. Totally embarrassing.

When we walked into the room, Alberta was already in her seat. Today she was wearing a purple bowling shirt. The name *Loreen* was stitched above a pocket. She matched it with a pair of pink stretch pants. Even though I barely glanced at her, Farley whispered in my ear, 'You like her.'

'Do not.'

'Do.'

'Do not.'

'Do.'

'Do not.'

'Do.' Et cetera, et cetera.

I sat beside Ambrose, who was wearing his ugly pom-pom hat.

'What's your name again?' he asked.

'Henry.'

'Henry what?'

I hesitated. 'Henry Larsen.'

'*O* or *E*?'

My neck muscles tensed. All it would take is a Google search – 'Larsen Port Salish' – and they'd find out everything.

'*O*,' I lied.

'Shore, early, nearly, sly, real, hole, heal, shone, share, shale, shy, rye, hen, hay, hare, has.'

I looked at him blankly.

'Duh. They're anagrams,' he said, like it was obvious. 'Using some of the letters in your name.'

'Oh.'

'Ambrose is a Scrabble champion,' Parvana piped up, stroking his arm.

'Oh.'

'I'm ranked twelfth in BC.'

'Oh.'

Mr Jankovich entered. 'Henry, nice to have you back. Let's get started.'

These are the questions I remember:

1) *What volcano is on the island of Sicily?* (Mount Etna – we all knew that one, but Shen buzzed in first.)
2) *What is the capital of Sicily?* (Palermo. Koula.)
3) *Sicily is surrounded by what body of water?* (The Mediterranean Sea. Answered by yours truly.)
4) *This actor has played Jack Sparrow, Ichabod Crane, and Gilbert Grape.* (Johnny Depp. You can guess who answered that one.)

There was also a series of 'Who Am I?' questions. We kept getting a new clue until we could figure it out.

Clue A: I grew up in Monroeville, Alabama.

Clue B: I was a tomboy.

Clue C: I was good friends with another literary icon, Truman Capote.

Clue D: I won the Pulitzer Prize for Fiction in 1961.

Jerome buzzed in after the fourth clue and gave the right answer: Harper Lee, the author of *To Kill a Mockingbird*. Before I knew it, the bell rang and it was time to leave.

It wasn't the absolute worst way to pass an hour.

After school, Farley followed me out the front doors and fell into step beside me. 'I thought you lived up the hill,' I said.

'I do.'

'Then why are you walking this way?'

'I'm hoping you'll invite me over.'

'I can't,' I said. We hadn't invited *anyone* over since we'd moved in.

'Why not?'

There were a million white lies I could have told, like, 'I have way too much homework,' or, 'My dad's home sick.'

Instead I said, 'The place is a mess.'

Lame.

Farley just grinned. 'Not a problem. I love messes!'

So Farley walked with me to our apartment. We started out on tree-lined residential streets. Then, after a few blocks, we turned left onto Broadway. We walked past four greengrocers, five coffee shops, three bookstores, and a gazillion sushi restaurants. We passed the billiard hall, where men in sweater-vests stood outside, speaking in Greek and drinking coffee from tiny cups. Farley was trying to tell me the entire story line from Season 1 of *Battlestar Galactica*, but I tuned him out.

Then I saw the Crazy Lady up ahead. She was outside the Vietnamese restaurant, wearing a purple dress, red kneesocks, and hot pink Crocs. She sang tunelessly while strumming on a plastic dollar-store guitar.

The Crazy Lady is there most days when I walk home from school, and the sight of her always makes me queasy.

'C'mon,' I said to Farley, 'let's cross here.' I didn't tell him we'd have to cross back a block later. I do this all the time to avoid the Crazy Lady.

When we got to our dingy gray building, my stomach was in knots. I took Farley up the back stairs so we wouldn't run into Mr Atapattu. I unlocked the door, and we stepped inside.

Suddenly I felt ashamed. The beige carpeting is covered in burn marks. The white walls haven't been white for years. Everything looks dingy and worn. Plus, we brought all the furniture from our three bedroom house and tried to fit it into a one bedroom den, so it's jammed with stuff that's too big for the rooms. You have to squeeze your way past the big brown leather couch and the big brown leather La-Z-Boy and the big oak coffee table to get to the galley kitchen.

But Farley just said, 'Wow, what a cool apartment!' Then he made a beeline for the shelf that held my PS3 games. He grabbed *Call of Duty 4* off the shelf. 'Wanna play?'

'Sure.'

As I loaded up the game, he said, 'What happened in here?' He pointed to a particularly large burn mark on the carpet, which we'd tried to cover with the coffee table.

'Rumor has it, the previous tenant had a meth lab,' I told him. 'He got caught because he started a fire one day.'

'Wow. You're living in a former drug den!' He sounded impressed.

Confession: Playing *Call of Duty 4* with Farley was fun. I hadn't played with a real live human being in ages. After a while, Farley said, 'I need to use your facilities.' It took me a moment to realize he meant the bathroom. I felt ashamed again because my dad and I haven't cleaned in there once since we moved in. I might keep my own room neat and tidy, but cleaning toilets is not my thing. Also, the toilet seat has a crack in it – if you need to sit down, you have to be very careful or risk getting your bum pinched.

Sure enough, a few minutes later I heard a yelp. But

when I went down the hall to investigate, Farley wasn't in the bathroom anymore.

He was in my bedroom.

My heart started pounding. *Where else had he been? What else had he seen?*

He was staring at my Great Dane poster. 'You're a GWF fan, too!' he exclaimed. 'This is incredible. We have so much in common, we could practically be related. Separated at birth or what!' I was speechless. There were so many ways that this made no sense. 'Except *my* favorite is Vlad the Impaler,' he continued.

'Vlad the Impaler?' I blurted. 'Are you nuts? That guy is pure evil.'

'Exactly! Every time he steps into the ring, you know it's gonna get interesting. Vlad means drama. Did you see last week, when he clotheslined Jett Turbo?'

'Duh, of course I saw it!'

We argued for a few more minutes about the Great Dane versus Vlad the Impaler, then Farley saw the time on my alarm clock. 'Yikes, I've got to go. Maria will start worrying.'

'Is Maria your mom?' I asked as we headed back to the living room.

'No, she's my nanny.'

I laughed because I thought he was joking.

'My parents live in Hong Kong. Maria lives here, with me. She's from the Philippines.'

'You're serious? You don't live with your parents?'

He nodded. 'They bought the house here two years ago cos they wanted me to go to school in Canada. And also because having property here is a good investment. Maria was my nanny in Hong Kong, too, so she moved here with me.' He grabbed his backpack and slung it over his shoulder. 'That's something else we have in common.'

'What?'

'We're both onlies.'

I looked at him blankly.

'I'm an only child; you're an only child.'

'Oh. Yeah.'

Once he was gone, I had to sit down.

In Port Salish, Mom had an entire wall devoted to family photographs: Jesse, tall and skinny and brown-haired like Mom, and me, short and stocky with bright red hair like Dad, burying Dad up to his neck in sand at the beach; Jesse, Mom, and me around the fire on one of our camping trips; Jesse and me and Dad holding up an enormous salmon we'd caught fishing; plus all the ugly school portraits that tracked us through the years.

Dad and I haven't unpacked those pictures yet. They're in our storage locker downstairs. In fact, unless you know about the shoebox, there's hardly any evidence in our apartment that Jesse ever existed.

This is fine by me.

After all, if your brother is dead, you technically don't have a brother anymore.

So I guess I didn't lie to Farley when I said 'Yeah.'

I *am* an only child. Jesse saw to that.

11:00 p.m.

INTRIGUING FACT: Cremations were done as far back as the Stone Age. They just burned their corpses on open fires.

These days, most cremations are done in computer-controlled steel ovens. I know because I've read all about it online. A body is put into a coffinlike container made of particleboard, then slid into the chamber like a really big roast beef or something. Temperatures reach around 1000°! The corpse takes about one and a half hours to burn.

When it's all done, about three to five pounds of bone fragments remain. Those bone fragments are put into a 'cremulator,' a machine that grinds them into ashes.

Some people buy a nice urn to hold a loved one's ashes. Other people sprinkle them into the ocean, or under a special tree. Some, like *Star Trek* creator Gene Rodenberry, have their ashes shot into outer space. Seriously, he did that.

Jesse's ashes are under my dad's bed.

I guess that makes us sound like awful people. But, really, we have no idea what to do with him. Put him in an urn and stick him in the living room, so we have to be reminded of him and what he did *every single time* we're in there? No, thanks. Sprinkle him in the ocean, so he can be eaten by fish? So that maybe a tiny bit of Jesse could be served to me one night in my salmon? No way. Bury his ashes in a cemetery? No. Jesse was mildly claustrophobic; that would be cruel.

So, for now, he lives under Dad's bed in a shoebox. It's kind of like purgatory, I guess. Not heaven, not hell, but a place in between.

Come to think of it, I guess we're living in purgatory, too.

Cecil was wearing a Grateful Dead T-shirt today. He's a walking, talking hippie stereotype.

'I was worried about you when you didn't show up last week,' he said once I'd sat down.

'I wasn't feeling well,' I lied.

'If you can't make it, leave a message with the front desk, OK?'

'OK.'

Then he put his feet up on the desk. His big toe poked through a hole in one of his purple-and-yellow striped socks. He tented his hands under his chin and looked at me intently, waiting for me to 'start the dialogue.' ('Start the dialogue' is another one of his favorite expressions.)

The thing is, I was one step ahead of him. In last period, I'd made a list of topics to discuss, so that it would look like I was opening up; but they were safe topics, things that wouldn't give him an opportunity to ask leading questions about IT. So I told him about the Reach For The Top Team ('Great that you're getting involved, Henry, great'), and I told him a little bit about Farley ('Holy Moly, you have a friend already! Fantastic.'). Then I told him about the Crazy Lady.

'She's missing a lot of her teeth,' I said. 'And she sings

these made-up songs . . . Her voice is terrible. And her guitar is plastic. It's from a dollar store.'

'She makes you uncomfortable.'

'She makes me *sad*. I keep thinking, was she always like this? Or did something happen to her along the way? Maybe she has a husband somewhere, and kids. Do they know where she is? Do they know she's lost her marbles?'

'Some people fall through the cracks in the system.'

'Well, they shouldn't. There shouldn't *be* any cracks.'

'No. There shouldn't.' Then he leaned forward in his chair and looked me in the eye. 'Henry, your mom is in good hands.'

I felt a flash of anger. 'Who said anything about my mom? I'm telling you about the Crazy Lady!'

Cecil means well. But he keeps trying to find meaning in things that have no meaning.

I suspect that he's smoked a lot of pot.

'Have you started writing in your journal yet?' he asked, changing the subject.

'A little,' I said. 'But only cos you said I had to.'

'I didn't say you had to. I just thought it might be helpful.'

'Well, it isn't.'

'I'm sorry to hear that.'

'It's dumb.' I was still feeling mad about the Crazy Lady.

'No one's forcing you to do it, Henry.'

'Then maybe I'll stop.'

'OK. If that's what you want.'

'You have no idea what I want.'

'I didn't say I did.'

'Well, good. Because you don't.'

'What *do* you want?'

I want time to rewind back a year. I want to change the course of history. ~~I want to change what I did the night of April 30.~~

'I want our session to be over because it's boring and you're stupid,' I said.

If I'd hurt his feelings, he didn't let it show. He just said, 'OK. I'm going to grant you your wish.' He stood up. 'Bye, Henry. See you next week.' Then he started sorting through a bunch of papers on his desk, acting like I wasn't even there.

Not very professional, if you ask me. I bet he's going to charge the province for the whole hour, too, even though we had a full ten minutes left.

I should write his bosses a letter and tell them to dock his pay.

3:00 a.m.

I just had *both* of my recurring nightmares. Call it a two-for-one special.

● ● ●

In the first dream, I'm hiding in the yellow tube slide and I can hear Jesse's cries. Then that one morphs into the second dream, and I'm suddenly at the scene of the crime, and I can't figure out who I should help first.

Half the time, I pick Scott. I use SpongeBob SquarePants Band-Aids to try to stop his bleeding, and no matter how many I use, the blood keeps pouring out of his chest.

Half the time, I pick Jesse. A piece of my brother's head lies on the corridor floor, by a bank of lockers. It's a neat break, like a piece from a porcelain doll. I gently pick it up. I line up the piece of his head that I've found with the part that is still on his body, trying not to look at his brain, which is on full display. Then I pull out a bottle of glue and glue my brother back together.

'Thanks,' Jesse says with a smile, 'You're not such a worthless turd after all.'

Then his smile falters because the glue doesn't hold. It's like the nightmare version of *Humpty Dumpty*.

All the king's horses and all the king's men
Couldn't put Jesse together again.

Wednesday, February 13

At the end of Home Ec today, Mrs Bardus announced that we would be starting a new unit next week. 'Cooking and nutrition,' she said. 'There aren't enough cooking stations for you to work on your own.'

I knew what she was going to say next, and I dreaded it. I tried to adopt a nonchalant, preoccupied look as she said, 'Please pick a partner. Let me know who you're working with on your way out.'

As the new kid, I knew my status. I was on the lowest rung of the ladder. So I waited patiently, figuring that when the other kids were paired off, I'd get the person on the second-lowest rung. My money was on Paula Peters. She's super shy, and her shoulders always have a dusting of dandruff. But she was snapped up right away by the girl sitting next to her.

Then I noticed that I wasn't the only one aiming for a nonchalant, preoccupied look. Alberta was, too. She tugged awkwardly on the sleeve of her oversized man's suit jacket, which she wore over a knee-length T-shirt and a pair of thick red-and-black polka-dot tights. She wasn't approaching anyone, and no one was approaching her.

This surprised me. I'd just assumed she had a ton of friends.

Kids were pairing off fast. And I must have had a

temporary brain fart because I suddenly heard myself saying, 'Alberta, would you be my partner?'

She rolled her eyes. 'Whatevs.'

'Is that a yes?'

'Duh.'

'Would you just say yes or no?'

'God! Yes, OK? Quit bugging me.'

Rude.

Thursday, February 14

We wrote haiku in English today. They're super-short poems, unrhymed – first line, five syllables; second line, seven syllables; third line, five syllables. Because it was Valentine's Day, Mr Schell asked us to write one that reflected the occasion. I got nine out of ten.

Haiku
by Henry K. Larsen

Valentine's Day means
Candy if you are in love,
Nothing if you're not.

Here's the one I didn't submit.

Charmed by your horse-laugh,
Your clothes, which smell of mothballs,
Your lazy left eye.

Friday, February 15

I was at my locker this morning when Farley burst through the doors at the end of the hall. 'Guess what! Guess what!' he shouted as he tore up to me, so that every single person in the corridor turned to look.

'What?'

'Guess!' He set his briefcase down. He was so excited, he was bouncing up and down on the balls of his feet.

'Farley. How can I possibly guess—'

'The GWF is coming to Seattle! The GWF is coming to Seattle!' Spittle was forming fast and furious at the corners of his mouth.

A tingle of excitement shot up my spine. 'When?' I asked.

'April 30th.'

I almost fell over. April 30th was the anniversary of the night of the Other Thing. I swear I could suddenly smell plastic and pee.

'Tickets start at twenty bucks US, but I think we should try to get good seats, right?' Farley was saying. 'The best seats!'

I couldn't answer because my tongue felt thick and heavy in my mouth.

'Imagine seeing Vlad the Impaler live! Imagine seeing the Great Dane! Imagine seeing Vlad drop someone with his Double Ax Handle!' Farley linked his hands together and spun around, swinging his arms to demonstrate—

And hit Troy square in the back.

At first, Troy looked more shocked than angry. 'What the hell, 'tard?'

'Tard. That was one of Scott's favorite insults, too. It's what he called my brother whenever he got tired of Ballsack.

Suddenly I was back on a sidewalk in downtown Port Salish, walking with Jesse. It was two summers ago, and Jesse was in a good mood because he'd just ordered a workout bench and weights from the Sears Outlet with money he'd saved from mowing lawns. I was in a good mood because I was only eleven going on twelve, and it was still fun to hang out downtown with my older brother.

'I'm going to start pumping iron,' he said to me. 'I'm going to get muscles as big as the Great Dane's.'

'Can I pump iron?'

'Maybe. Only if I'm around.' His mind was whirring. 'I'm going to buy a punching bag next. Or maybe I'll take karate lessons. I wonder how long it takes to get your black belt.'

'Why do you want your black belt?'

He didn't answer my question. 'Want to get some ice cream? My treat.'

I remember thinking what an awesome brother I had.

Then Scott drove by with some of his friends. Like everyone else, I knew about the nickname Scott had given Jesse. I knew Jesse hadn't had a great first year in high school. But until that day, I didn't understand how bad it was.

'Hey, it's Jodie's brother,' I said.

Jesse's face went blank. He grabbed my hand and started walking faster. 'Don't make eye contact,' he said.

The car slowed down. Then Scott yelled out the passenger window, 'Hey, Jesse! Ya 'tard!' Something came sailing out the window. It was a half-full can of Coke, aimed at Jesse's head.

The can just missed its target. It landed on the sidewalk in front of us. Coke splashed onto Jesse's pants as the car squealed away.

We didn't go for ice cream. We just walked straight home. I remember that Jesse was really embarrassed. And I remember that I was embarrassed, too, because I suddenly knew with total certainty that my brother was not cool. My brother was the kid the other kids made fun of.

I think that was the day I stopped looking up to him. I think that was the day I started to feel a little bit ashamed of him.

It was hard to write those last two sentences.

● ● ●

Anyway.

I'd buried that memory really deep. So the fact that it was playing itself out in my head all of a sudden, in full Technicolor, really knocked the wind out of me, and maybe that's why I didn't try to stop what happened next. Troy grabbed Farley and got his buddy, the one named Mike, to hold open Farley's locker door. 'You ever touch me again, Slant-Eyes, you are dead.'

Farley was squirming and shouting, 'It was an accident! I swear!'

Troy shoved Farley into his locker. Mike slammed the door shut. Farley kept shouting; it was just a little more muffled. The one named Josh clicked Farley's lock into place. Then the three of them sauntered away, laughing.

I've seen kids get stuffed into lockers on TV shows and in movies, but never in real life. It didn't look as funny in real life.

'99–10–12!' Farley yelled through the slats in the door. '99–10–12!'

It took me a few seconds to realize he was shouting his locker combination. I finally unfroze and spun his lock around. I yanked open the door. Farley stepped out, adjusting his glasses.

'He's a psycho,' said Farley.

'A racist psycho,' I added.

'He tried to kill Ambrose once.'

'Get out.'

'It's true. They went to the same elementary school. Troy and his friends slipped a peanut into Ambrose's sandwich, even though they knew he was allergic. He almost died.'

The warning bell rang. 'That's awful,' I said.

'Aw, fudge.' Farley was looking down at his button-up shirt. The pocket was torn almost completely off, exposing the plastic pocket protector and pens underneath. 'He tore my shirt.' His glasses fogged up, and I realized he was fighting tears.

'Do you want to go tell the principal?' I asked.

Farley looked at me like I was mental. He didn't have to say a word; I knew exactly what he meant. Going to the principal might make things better; or it might make things worse.

Jesse went to the principal once. The principal spoke to Scott. And do you know what happened? Scott just got better at covering his tracks. And Jesse got branded as a snitch.

Farley took a cloth handkerchief out of his pants pocket and blew into it loudly. He sounded like a Canada goose.

'C'mon,' he said. 'I don't want to break my perfect attendance record.' He stuffed the handkerchief back into his pocket, and we headed to class.

● ● ●

82

What I like most about Farley is that he's like a rubber ball. No matter how hard you throw him, he bounces right back.

What I hate most about Farley is that he's like a rubber ball. No matter how hard you throw him, he bounces right back.

'So listen,' he said the moment class got out, 'talk to your dad. See if he'll take us to Seattle – because my parents can't, obviously, they're in Hong Kong. And Maria doesn't have her license. We could drive down and back the same day. Plus,' he continued, stopping his rapid-fire monologue only to take a deep breath, 'we need money to buy the tickets. And for gas and food and stuff.' He started to bounce on the balls of his feet. 'I broke down the costs on an Excel spreadsheet last night. They're based on three of us going. Me, you, and your dad.'

He knelt down and opened up his briefcase in the hallway. Then he handed me a sheet of paper.

Three tickets –	$200.00
Gas –	$50.00
Food –	$50.00
Souvenirs –	$100.00
Total –	**$400.00**

'That's a ton of money,' I told him.

'The tickets might be a bit less, but I had to factor in all those dumb service charges. And I *know* I'm not leaving there without a GWF T-shirt and a Vlad the Impaler poster.'

'I don't have any money.'

'Me, neither. My parents make a lot of money in Hong Kong, but they're cheapskates. They give Maria just enough for our expenses.'

We'd arrived in English class. Farley sat beside me. 'Would your parents maybe lend you the money, and then we can figure out a way to pay them back?'

I looked away. How could I explain that my parents didn't have any money? *Well, Farley, my mom can't work because she's in a loony bin, and our place is still for sale in Port Salish because no one wants to live in a murderer's house. Oh, and since criminal charges were never laid against my brother because you can't charge a dead person, the Marlins have launched a civil suit against my parents, claiming 'wrongful death'. If they win, we might owe them a lot of money that we don't have.*

Yeah, no.

'Just ask them over the weekend, OK? We *have* to go see this! We have to!'

Our teacher entered, and I thought that would shut Farley up. But he just kept whispering loudly, 'Please! Please!' even after Mr Schell started the lesson.

'Henry Larsen, tell your friend Mr Wong to zip it,' Mr Schell said.

But even that didn't shut Farley up. He just kept whispering, over and over and over, 'Pleasepleaseplease pleasepleasepleasepleasepleaseplease—'

'Fine!' I said. 'I'll ask.'

Even though I knew I never would.

Later

I hate Cecil.

When I showed up at his office this afternoon, he said, 'What do you say we go for a walk? It's a beautiful day.'

Leaving the office seemed very 'un-psychologist-like,' but it *was* a beautiful day – sunny after weeks of rain – so I said OK.

Once we were outside, he told me a long boring story about the matzo ball soup his mom would make when he had a cold and how good it made him feel. I was like *yawn*, but I nodded to be polite.

'Why don't you tell me a happy memory about your family?' he said.

I have plenty of good memories about my family. But maybe I wanted to get a rise out of Cecil because I said, 'We loved a good fart joke.'

He didn't miss a beat. 'Great. Tell me one.'

'Confucius say, man who farts in church must sit in his own pew.'

He laughed. 'That's pretty good.'

So I told him another one. 'What's invisible and smells like carrots? The Easter Bunny's farts.'

Cecil obviously likes toilet humor cos he laughed really hard, and I guess it made me feel good because I kept on going.

'Whenever we go to my Pop-Pop and Grams's in Ontario, Pop-Pop *always* toots at the supper table. Like, loud.'

'Holy Moly.'

'He's sixty per cent deaf, and I guess he thinks that if he can't hear it, we can't either. But, of course, we can. And we have to try *so hard* not to laugh. Mom winds up snorting water up her nose. And Jesse and I have to squeeze each other's knees really hard under the table—' I stopped.

I'd broken two rules. I'd spoken Jesse's name aloud. And worse, I'd talked about him like he was still alive.

'Tell me another good memory.'

'No, thanks.'

'Please?'

'No, thanks.'

'Henry,' he began, 'it's OK to talk about your brother. It's healthy.'

'I Am. An Only Child,' I answered in Robot-Voice.

'No, you're not. You had a brother, and you loved him.

And I bet you still love him, even if you're really angry with him, too. Those conflicting emotions are totally normal.'

I didn't answer.

'Your dad told me what happened in the park a month before Jesse died—'

'System Meltdown!' I shouted in Robot-Voice. 'System Meltdown! System Meltdown!' People on the sidewalk were turning to stare.

'It's OK, Henry. Calm down—'

'System Meltdown!' I kept shouting as I spun in circles, flailing my arms.

'Why don't we go back to the office—'

'System Meltdown!' I shouted again, then I ran away from Cecil as fast as my pygmy legs and my wobblies would carry me, which wasn't very fast. But Cecil didn't take up the chase. I guess he figured it wouldn't look good – an old guy in a ponytail trying to tackle a kid.

When I got home, Dad still wasn't there, so I went into his room and pulled the shoebox out from under his bed.

'Shithead,' I whispered. 'Thanks for ruining my life.'

Then I changed into my pajamas and ate four peanut butter and jelly sandwiches in a row.

Saturday, February 16

INTRIGUING FACT: Weekends didn't exist till the 1940s. Henry Ford was one of the first bosses to give his workers two days off in a row, in 1926; he figured people buying his Model T's needed leisure time to drive them.

Before IT happened, I loved weekends. My family was good at them. In nice weather, we'd pack up the car and go camping or fishing. In bad weather, we'd bake bread and cookies and play board games and, of course, watch *Saturday Night Smash-Up*.

These days, weekends are torture. Today, for example, Dad spent a lot of time in bed with a 'cold'. I'm pretty sure this was code for 'hangover'. Usually he just drinks beer, but on Friday night he brought home a bottle of Jack Daniel's, and I noticed this morning that it was half-full.

Since he wasn't feeling well, I did some chores around the apartment. I even put on rubber gloves and plugged my nose and scrubbed out the toilet, for the first time since we moved in. Gross. Then I lugged a garbage bag full of dirty clothes to the laundry room in the basement. All the way down in the painfully slow elevator, I fantasized about seeing the *GWF Smash-Up Live!* in Seattle. But we could never afford it. I know I have to let it go.

When I got to the laundry room, all of the washing

machines were full. One of them had finished its cycle, so I pulled the clothes out and placed them on the counter. Believe me, I had no desire to touch someone else's clothes – especially not someone else's *frilly undergarments*. But when something fell on the floor, I had no choice but to pick it up. It happened to be a very red BRA with big huge CUPS, and just as I was placing it on the counter, I heard, 'Are you fondling my brassiere?'

Karen. She was standing in the doorway to the laundry room, arms crossed, smirking.

In an instant, my face felt like it was on fire, and I knew that even my freckles were blushing. 'I was just emptying the machine so I could use it,' I said, hating her.

'You shouldn't do that, you know,' she said as she started to toss her stuff into a dryer. 'No one likes a stranger pawing through their clothes.'

'I wasn't pawing!'

'Could've fooled me,' she said, smirking again.

Then, to make a crap day crappier, Mr Atapattu entered the laundry room. 'Henry, greetings! How are you?'

'Fine,' I muttered as Mr Atapattu opened a dryer and started removing his clothes.

'He was pawing through my underwear,' Karen said, and it dawned on me that she was enjoying herself.

'I was not!! I was just emptying the machine!'

Mr Atapattu tilted his head toward Karen. 'Hello. I don't believe we've met. Suresh Atapattu, 213.'

'Karen Vargas. 311.'

They shook hands.

'I was just telling Harry here—' Karen began.

'Henry!' I said, louder than I meant to. I was dying to get out of there. I'd shoved our clothes into the machine and added detergent, and I fumbled for a loonie in my pocket.

'Excuse me, I was just telling *Henry* that he shouldn't remove someone else's clothes from one of the machines.'

'Oh, I don't know about that,' said Mr Atapattu. 'It can be very annoying when people don't empty the machines promptly.'

'True, but still, touching their clothes – it's an invasion of privacy.'

'But that is the price you pay for living in a building with shared laundry facilities,' Mr Atapattu replied. 'A little less privacy.'

Karen crossed her arms and pursed her lips. 'So you're saying just because some of us can't afford to live in a building with an ensuite laundry, we should have less privacy?'

'You misinterpret my words. I simply mean that, when a large number of people have to use common facilities, rules must be bent to accommodate everyone, isn't that right, Henry?'

But I'd managed to get the machine started, and I was already halfway out the door. I could hear them arguing as I stood waiting for the elevator.

'If you don't want anyone else to touch your things, you should be here when your laundry is done.'

'I was ten minutes late! So sue me!'

I couldn't take it any longer, so I walked up the stairs instead.

Later, when it was time to flip our clothes into a dryer, I approached the laundry room like a sniper in *Call of Duty 4*. I poked my head in to make sure the coast was clear. It wasn't. Karen was there, and she was posting a big handwritten sign over the washing machines that said PLEASE DO NOT REMOVE OTHER TENANTS' CLOTHING. Then she picked up her hamper, which was full of dry clothes.

I panicked. No way did I want to have to talk to her again about her *undergarments*, or anything else for that matter, so I hurried back down the corridor. But instead of going *right* toward the stairs, I went *left* toward the elevator, and it wasn't till I was passing the storage lockers that I realized my mistake. The elevator would take forever to show up. Not only would Karen catch up to me, but we'd have to ride up in that cramped space *together*. With her brassieres!

Then I remembered that the key to our storage locker was on my key ring. I quickly opened our unit and slipped inside. The lockers are basically just floor-to-ceiling metal cages, meaning anyone can see in, but I hid behind some boxes, and luckily Karen didn't notice me as she passed.

I meant to leave as soon as she was gone. But then I started reading the labels on the boxes: KITCHEN, EXTRA LINENS, PHOTO ALBUMS.

JESSE & HENRY.

I only meant to take a little peek. But before I knew it, I was going through every single item: our old ratty blankets (his was called Softie, mine was called Blankie); all of our report cards; the knitted blueberry hat Jesse wore as a baby, which was then handed down to me; some of our artwork, including a fire truck that Jesse had painted when he was six. He'd signed it STEVE. Suddenly I was laughing because I remembered that, for a month in first grade, he had insisted on being called Steve. We never knew why, but it became a favorite family story.

Even our Lego drivers' licenses were in there. I'd been seven and Jesse had been nine when we went on that trip – the trip of a lifetime, as far as we were concerned. Mom and Dad had scrimped and saved to take us to California for a week. We'd gone to the San Diego Zoo and to SeaWorld and, of course, to Legoland, where we drove Lego cars and got Lego drivers' licenses.

Two envelopes were in the box, one marked HENRY, one marked JESSE. Each of them held a lock of our hair from our first haircuts – Jesse's dark brown, mine bright red. Holding Jesse's hair sent a chill up my spine because, aside from what's in the shoebox, I was holding all that's left of him.

And then, stupidly, I brought Softie up to my face and breathed deep, and it was the worst thing I could have done because I could *smell* Jesse, I swear I could, and suddenly I was sobbing like crazy. I heard the elevator doors open, and I stuffed Softie into my mouth. My body kept shuddering, but no sounds came out. Mr Atapattu walked by, but he didn't see me. Finally, after he'd gone back upstairs, and after I was sure the coast was clear, I forced myself to shove everything back into the box. I left the storage locker and headed to the laundry room to get our clothes from the dryer.

Mr Atapattu had stuck a new handwritten sign under Karen's. This one said IF YOU DO NOT REMOVE YOUR CLOTHES IN A TIMELY FASHION (WHICH IS COMMON COURTESY), THEY WILL BE REMOVED FOR YOU!!!

Sometimes I truly hate living in this building.

Midnight

Questions I would like to ask Jesse:

1) Why did you do it, you dick?
2) Did you ever stop to think about what it would do to the rest of us?
3) Where did you put the *Settlers of Catan* game, because none of us can find it anywhere?
4) Why did you do it, you dick?

Monday, February 18

Trying to tell Farley 'no' is like trying to tell a brand-new puppy not to pee in the house: impossible. The moment he saw me in Math, he made a beeline for me, sliding into the desk next to mine.

'*There* you are! I've been looking for you all day!'

And I've been avoiding you all day! I wanted to say.

'So? Did you talk to your dad?'

'No,' I told him.

His face dropped. 'Why not?'

I took a deep breath. 'It's a long story.'

'I've got time.'

So I told Farley a portion of the truth, to get him off my back. 'We don't have any money. My dad can barely afford to pay our rent these days, and my mom isn't working . . .'

Farley studied me with his big magnified eyes. 'Where is your mom, anyway?'

'Excuse me?'

'She's not living with you.'

'Who told you that?'

'No one. I just noticed. There was no girl stuff at your place.'

'You were snooping?'

'No. It was simple observation. Only men's shoes, no makeup in the bathroom, that sort of thing.'

The tips of my ears felt hot. 'This is so not your business,' I said to him, just as Ms Wrightson entered the room.

'I didn't say it to make you mad,' Farley said. 'And, anyway, it's no big deal. Did you know that thirty-eight per cent of marriages end in divorce before their thirtieth year? I learned that doing a project in Socials—'

'My parents aren't divorced!' I said, more loudly than I meant to. A few kids looked in our direction.

'Farley and Henry, eyes to the front and mouths shut,' Ms Wrightson said in her dreary monotone. 'Fasten your seatbelts, kids, because today we enter the exciting world of trigonometry.'

Farley tried to get my attention all through class – staring at me, clearing his throat, even poking me in the arm with his compass once. But I wouldn't give him the satisfaction. I just followed Ms Wrightson's instructions and kept my mouth shut.

The moment Math was over, I jumped up and headed for the door, but Farley was right on my heels.

'Where are you going? We have to meet in the foyer.'

'What for?'

'Duh, our Reach For The Top game!'

I'd totally forgotten. Five minutes later, Mr Jankovich

was herding all of us to the bus stop. We piled on to the number 99. Thankfully Jerome started to quiz Farley, so he stopped bugging me about the GWF.

We played against Borden Secondary on the east side. And guess what: We won!! The other team was really good, especially this girl named Phoebe, who must've scored over half of their points. But their weakness was Canadian History. Lucky for us, Jerome is a Canadian History buff (who knew such a person existed). In the final round, we got a 'Point Team Question.' This means, the team that answers the *first* ten-point question correctly gets dibs on answering the next *three* questions, and since all of the questions were about Sir Wilfrid Laurier, one of Canada's prime ministers in the Dark Ages, Jerome nailed them. We edged out Borden by twenty points.

Everyone was in a good mood on the way home. The bus was crowded, and most of us had to stand. Some of my teammates found room in the back. I wound up at the front, with Alberta.

She was wearing a pair of men's plaid pants and a zip-up sweater with a deer on the back that smelled like mothballs and cheese. I know this because she's a good three inches taller than me, and every time the bus lurched, my nose got pressed into her shoulder.

When I looked up, she was gazing right at me.

'Intriguing outfit,' I said.

'Thanks,' she replied, choosing to take it as a compliment. 'I get all my clothes at the Sally Ann or Value Village. I call it the Recycled Look.'

'Good game today,' I said, even though she'd got only two questions right, the answers of which were Lady Gaga and Paris Hilton.

'Yeah, thanks.'

Then the bus jerked to a halt, and we both grabbed on to the same pole to keep our balance. Her hand was directly above mine, so close that her pinky touched my thumb.

Not that I'm reading anything into this. I'm sure it was totally an accident. She probably didn't even realize our digits had made contact.

Still, she didn't move her hand for the rest of the way home.

And neither did I.

When I got home, it was almost six. I could hear Dad before I could see him. He was on the phone. '. . . Curly red hair, about five feet two inches . . .'

I almost shouted out, *Five feet* three *inches!*

'I *know* it's only been a couple of hours. But you don't understand—'

I walked into the living room. He was pacing and

running one hand through his hair over and over, like he does when he's anxious or stressed. His work boots were still on his feet, and they were tracking mud all over the carpet.

His eyes met mine. 'Never mind. I'm sorry. He just came in.'

He hung up the phone. I knew right away I was in trouble when he said, 'Henry Kaspar Larsen!' He only calls me by my full name when he's really mad. 'I was worried sick.' His voice caught. He grabbed me and pulled me into a bear hug, so tight I could hardly breathe.

'I'm sorry,' I said into his flannel shirt. 'I had a Reach For The Top game. I forgot to tell you.'

Dad let me go, but he kept his hands on my shoulders. 'Don't *ever* do that again, don't *ever* forget to tell me – do you understand?!' He was shaking me now, and for a moment I almost felt scared. My dad's a big guy, not super-tall but beefy and strong.

'Dad, I'm sorry!'

He let me go and sank onto the couch. He put his head in his hands. His shoulders started heaving, and at first I thought he was laughing.

But he wasn't. He was crying. More like sobbing, actually.

Dad has always been an emotional guy. We used to make fun of him cos he'd get teary-eyed at almost anything on TV, including reruns of *Friends*. My mom used to say he was like a peppermint patty: hard outer shell but gooey in the middle.

This was different. I'd only seen him cry like this once before. It was about a week after Jesse's funeral. We'd been washing the dishes, and he suddenly sank to the floor and started bawling like a baby, for what felt like *hours*. My mom and I finally left him on the floor and went upstairs to escape the awful sound.

I'm not dumb. I knew what had been going through his mind when he came home and I wasn't there. Once you have a suicide in the family, it doesn't seem like such a stretch to believe that it could happen again. You start to think of it like a flu virus. It could spread.

So I sat down beside him, and I leaned into him and patted his bushy red hair, and pretty soon, I was crying, too, which made me feel like a dork because my tear ducts have been working overtime lately.

'I'm so sorry, Dad. I never meant to worry you. I love you.'

'I love you, too, Henry. I love you so much.'

After a while, we *both* started to feel like dorks. 'Do you think the Great Dane ever cries?' Dad asked as he blew his nose.

'Definitely.'

'What about Vlad the Impaler?'

'Never. His mother had his tear ducts removed when he was a baby.'

Dad laughed. 'We need to get you a cell phone.'

'Dad, we can't afford it.'

'We'll get the cheapest plan. I need to know I can get in touch.' He blew his nose again. 'I haven't done anything about supper.'

'That's OK. I'll make supper,' I said. I let him choose between the three meals I know how to make. 'Beans and wieners, scrambled eggs and wieners, or Kraft Dinner and wieners?'

'Beans and wieners sounds delicious.'

We ate in front of the TV. After dinner, I asked Dad to measure me, and guess what: I'm now five feet, three and three-quarter inches! Even Dad agreed it wasn't just my hair this time.

'Tell me when your next Reach For The Top tournament is,' he said when we were both standing by the bathroom sink, brushing our teeth. 'Not just so I won't worry – so I can come.'

And I almost started crying again because *that's* the dad I used to know. *That's* the dad I had up until June 1st, the guy who came to all our school concerts and sports days and plays.

And it made me feel *so good* to realize that *that* dad was still in there, somewhere.

But all I said was, 'I will, Dad. For sure.'

1:00 a.m.
Mr Atapattu is watching the Home Shopping Network again. They're advertising something called the Slanket.

1:30 a.m.
I'm pretty sure Alberta's pinky touched my thumb by accident.

Yup. Pretty sure.

Tuesday, February 19

INTRIGUING FACT: Cockroaches have been around for 350 million years. They can survive anything, even nuclear bombs. And they're extremely hard to get rid of.

Farley is like my own personal cockroach.

He sat across from me in the cafeteria today. 'To recap,' he began. 'We can't ask our parents for the money to go see the *GWF Smash-Up Live!* Correct?'

'Correct.'

'Which means—'

'We can't go.'

He shook his head. 'Henry, you disappoint me. It means we need to figure out a way to make the money.'

'Farley,' I said, trying to be patient, 'drop it. There's no way we can make that kind of money between now and the end of April.'

'Sure, there is. We have two and a half months. We'll get part-time jobs.'

'Like what? We're only thirteen.'

'We'll baby-sit.'

'Have you taken a baby-sitting course?'

'No.'

'Do you know anything about kids?'

'No.'

'Do you know anyone *with* kids?'

'No.'

'I rest my case.'

'What about odd jobs? We could put signs up around the neighborhood, do yard work, mow lawns – that sort of stuff.'

'Farley, it's *February*. Plus we'd need to have our own equipment.'

'Hey, nerds.' I glanced up. Alberta was heading our way, carrying a plate of fries with gravy. She looked almost normal today, in a pair of jeans and a pink T-shirt with brown lettering on the front. Then I read what it said: *If God Didn't Want Us to Eat Animals, He Wouldn't Have Made Them out of Meat.*

'Shove over,' she said as she slid in beside me. Her thigh brushed mine, and I was suddenly glad that the table covered the lower half of my body.

'Alberta, maybe you can help us,' Farley said.

I tried to signal to Farley to shut up.

'We're trying to figure out how to make four hundred bucks in two and a half months,' Farley told her.

'For what?'

'Nothing—' I started.

'The Global Wrestling Federation's *Smash-Up Live!* show is coming to Seattle at the end of April. Henry and I are huge fans.'

I waited for it.

She did not disappoint.

'*Ha-ha-ha-ha-ha-ha-HEEE-haw!*' she laughed. 'And you thought being on the Reach For The Top team was nerdy.'

'You did?' Farley asked, but Alberta kept laughing so I didn't have to respond.

'*Ha-ha-ha-ha-ha-ha-HEEE-haw!*' When she finally finished laughing, she dug into her fries, and I mean she really dug into them, shoveling them into her mouth like she hadn't eaten for a week. It was disgusting, yet oddly charming.

'Don't knock it till you've watched it,' Farley said to her. 'You might just change your mind.'

'Oh, I've watched once or twice. You do know it's totally fake?'

'So? It's not about that,' said Farley. 'They're amazing athletes. They really do get hurt out there.'

'It's like theater,' I added. 'It's exciting to watch. They create all these ongoing story lines, and all the wrestlers have distinct roles . . . It's like . . .' I said, searching for the words.

'Like a soap opera for guys,' Alberta said.

I thought about that for a moment. 'Yeah. I guess it is.'

'That makes a strange sort of sense,' she said. 'Like *The Young and the Restless*, but for the Y chromosomes.'

'Exactly,' said Farley, just as an empty pop can hit him on the side of the head.

Because Alberta and I were sitting across from him, we could see the culprit. Troy sat two tables behind us, with Mike and Josh. A teacher walking past stopped and glared at him. 'Oops, sorry,' Troy said with an apologetic grin. 'I was trying to get it into the recycling bin.'

The bin was directly behind Farley. 'Next time, walk over and place it in,' the teacher said, falling for Troy's story.

'Yes, Sir!' Troy replied. 'Sorry, Sir.'

Sometimes teachers are so dumb.

Farley didn't say a word. He just picked the can up from the floor, turned around, and stuffed it into the recycling bin, which was overflowing with cans and bottles.

'There's your answer,' said Alberta. We both looked at her, not getting it. 'You need to make four hundred bucks fast.' She pointed to the recycling bins. 'They get cleared out twice a week. If you go through them the day before, you could bring what you find to the recycling depot on Broadway and get back the deposits.'

Farley's eyes widened. 'And there's around,' he did the mental calculation, 'twenty recycling bins in the school . . . twelve hundred kids . . . If we get just twenty-five cans or bottles from each bin per week . . . what is it, like, ten cents a can or bottle? We stand to make fifty bucks per week!' He held up a hand to high-five Alberta. She obliged.

'You're welcome,' she said with a smug little grin.

'No,' I said. 'No way. We'd have to *garbage-pick*. In front of the *entire school*.'

'Not if we do it first thing in the morning, before the other kids show up,' Farley said. 'We can store everything in our lockers and bring it to the depot after school.' He started jotting down figures. 'They empty the bins on Tuesday and Thursday nights, so if we do rounds on Tuesday and Thursday mornings—'

'Not doing it.'

'Come on, Henry, it's easy money!'

'No! We'd look like total dorks.'

Alberta snorted. 'No offense,' she said, 'but you guys are GWF fans. You're *already* dorks.' Then she picked up her plate, held it up to her face, and licked off the remaining gravy, I kid you not. 'See you later.'

She started to walk away, then stopped. 'Hey, what has eight teeth and an IQ of 73?'

We shrugged.

'The first two rows of a wrestling crowd.'

I waited for it again.

'Ha-ha-ha-ha-ha-ha-HEEE-haw!'

Wednesday, February 20

I'm going to write it down to make it official: I will never, ever, *ever*, stoop to garbage-picking to make money, no matter how much Farley begs and pleads.

Which he is doing right now, in English class.

NEVER.

That was for Farley's benefit because he keeps trying to read over my shoulder.

FARLEY STINKS.

That was also for his benefit.

I'm so angry, I'm vibrating.

I showed up for my session with Cecil after school, and this skinny lady with short curly hair and bulgy eyes and a yellow T-shirt that said *Up with Life!* stepped into the waiting area. 'Henry Larsen?' she said.

'Yes,' I said.

'I'm Carol. Follow me.' And it wasn't till I was trapped in her office that she told me Cecil was home with the flu, but I could talk to her instead. I said, 'No, that's OK,' but she just launched right in. She looked at my file, and then she said, 'So your brother shot and killed a young man, then took his own life . . . Right, I remember hearing about it on the news.'

!!!!

Then she started scanning through her papers, barely even looking at me, and when she *did* look up, she looked at my wobblies!! And she said, 'Your file mentions that you've been putting on weight since this tragedy occurred. Do you use food as a comfort mechanism when you're feeling depressed?'

!!!!????

My furies exploded. I launched right into Robot-Henry. 'On My Planet. Wobblies Are a Sign. Of Status and Wealth.'

The expression on her face was priceless. Like she'd just swallowed a red-hot chili pepper.

'Why are you talking to me in that voice?'

'What Voice? What Do You Mean, Earthling? Explain Yourself or I Will. Zap You with My Ray Gun.'

She looked like she was going to poop in her pants. She started edging toward the door, and I couldn't help myself, I started robot-walking toward her. 'You Can Run, Earthling. But You Cannot Hide.'

Carol threw open the door and bolted down the hallway. I could hear her talking to the receptionist at the front desk. I picked up my backpack and walked out of her office. Carol froze when I entered the waiting area. 'You Are. A Shitty, Shitty Therapist,' I said in Robot-Voice. Then I left.

Next time I see Cecil, I will make it crystal clear: I talk to no one but him.

He may be a dud. But he's *my* dud.

Midnight

I can't believe Cecil wrote about my wobblies in his file!!!!

Saturday, February 23

INTRIGUING FACT: An omen is a sign that something lousy is about to happen. For example, some people believe that if a black cat crosses your path, or if you open an umbrella inside, or if a bird flies into your house, it will bring bad luck.

I had a kind of omen today. Except mine wasn't a bird in the house.

Mine was a woman in the apartment.

It was close to suppertime. I'd gone out for a long walk by myself to Jericho Beach, which is about a fifteen-minute walk from our place, partly because Dad had started working his way through the second half of that bottle of Jack Daniel's, and partly because I've decided I should try to get more exercise to deal with my wobblies. When I opened the door to our apartment, I heard a female voice.

My heart did a somersault. I almost said *Mom!* but even before I could form the word, I knew it wasn't Mom.

It was Karen. She was sitting on our couch, with her feet on our coffee table, wearing a low-cut black top that revealed way too much boobage. Dad sat across from her in his matching leather La-Z-Boy. They were each holding a glass of Jack Daniel's on the rocks.

'Henry, hi!' my dad said when he saw me, like everything

was totally normal, like this wasn't totally messed up. 'Karen dropped by with some of our mail.'

'The postie put it in my box yesterday instead of yours,' she said.

'She's been telling me all about her work in the movies. She's a hairstylist.'

'Well, I work mostly at a hairdressing school now,' she said. 'But I still occasionally do movies.'

'She's met a lot of celebrities,' Dad said.

'Didn't Mom want us to call her?' I asked.

Dad looked at me, puzzled. 'No, I don't think so. Hey, get this, Karen's met Tom Hanks—'

I turned around and walked out.

My furies crashed over me like a tidal wave. I was seeing black spots in front of my eyes. I was so mad, I forgot to grab my shoes, and I didn't realize it till I was standing outside the building in my socks, getting soaked because it was pouring rain. I turned to go back in, but I *couldn't* go back in because I'd left my key sitting on the hall table. I thought about buzzing our apartment, but that would totally defeat the point I was trying to make by storming out.

Five words ran through my head in a continuous loop: *How stupid is my dad??* Couldn't he see what Karen was doing? Couldn't he see that she was trying to sink her claws into him cos Mom wasn't around?

Then five new words took their place: *It is freezing out here!!*

'Henry – what is wrong?' It was Mr Atapattu, coming up the walk, carrying a bunch of grocery bags.

My teeth were chattering so much, I couldn't answer.

'Get inside,' he ordered, opening the door. 'Did you get locked out?'

'Yes,' I said.

'Without your shoes?'

'Yes.'

'I saw your father's truck out front. You couldn't buzz him?'

I just looked at my feet. My socks were oozing water.

Mr Atapattu studied me for a moment. 'Well,' he said. 'I'm glad you're here. The elevator is out of service again, and I could really use a hand with these bags.'

I helped him carry his groceries to his apartment. 'Thank you,' he said as he opened his door. 'Will you have a cup of tea with me? I made more *barfi* last night. And I can get you some dry socks.'

I didn't want to go into Mr Atapattu's place. But I was freezing. And I couldn't go home. And I couldn't go anywhere else without shoes.

I looked into his face. He didn't look like a child

molester or a murderer, and even if he was, well, it would serve Dad right.

So I said, 'OK.'

Mr Atapattu's place reeks of curry, which doesn't surprise me since I can smell it in my bedroom all the time. It's not a bad smell, it's just intense.

I peeled off my wet socks at the door. He showed me in to the living room, which is like a mirror image of ours only much more colorful, with bright patterned cushions and lampshades and rugs. 'Sit, sit,' he said. He hurried into his bedroom and returned with a thick pair of woolen socks. It was kind of weird, putting on an almost-stranger's socks, but I did it anyway. My feet immediately started to warm up.

'Here, put on my Slanket as well,' he said, and he handed me a big red blanket with sleeves.

'Did you buy this from the Home Shopping Network?' I asked.

'Yes. I am never disappointed with their products.' He smiled broadly, letting all of his teeth show. 'Notice a difference? I'm also using *Thirty Second Smile* to whiten my teeth!'

I put my arms through the Slanket. It was definitely cozy.

Mr Atapattu went into the kitchen to make tea. Unlike our place, his walls were covered with framed photos. I stood up to have a closer look. A lot of them were of an older woman who – there is no nice way to put this – was seriously ugly. I'm talking warts on her face and even a mustache.

My new cell phone started to ring. I knew it was Dad. I was mad at him, but I also didn't want to give him a heart attack. So I waited till it stopped ringing, then I texted him: *I'll come back when she's gone.*

He texted me back: *You are being silly.*

No, U r being silly, I typed.

Mr Atapattu came back in just as I was putting away my phone. He set a tray down on the coffee table and handed me a small cup with no handles. 'Chai,' he said. It smelled spicy.

'Who's that?' I asked, pointing at a photo of a young couple. She was wearing a colorful sari-type dress, and he was in a white shirt without a collar and matching white pants.

'That's my wife and me, on our wedding day,' he told me.

'That's you??' I said, leaning in for a closer look.

He laughed. 'Yes, that's me. Shocking, isn't it, that I was once young and handsome.'

'Where's your wife?'

'She died five years ago. Cancer.' He was quiet for a moment. 'That's her, a year before she died.' He pointed at the photo of the woman with the warts and the mustache, and yes, I felt like a jerk. Mr Atapattu sighed heavily. 'She was the love of my life.'

I didn't know what to say, so I had a sip of my tea. It was sweet and delicious. 'What about the car?' I asked, pointing at a photo of Mr Atapattu standing in front of a yellow cab.

He grinned. 'Chandrika.'

'Chandrika?'

'I named her after my favorite Sri Lankan female cricket player. Chandrika was my livelihood. I drove her for Black Top Cabs for over twenty years.'

'Are you retired?'

'I suppose I am. I have chronic back pain. So I sold Chandrika's license to a friend of mine.'

'Do you miss driving a cab?'

'Oh, yes. I loved it. I met many interesting people. Once I even drove Daniel and Henrik Sedin to a restaurant.'

'Daniel and Henrik Sedin from the Vancouver Canucks?'

He nodded. 'They were very good tippers. But enough about me,' he continued. 'Tell me all about you. What are your favorite subjects? Do you like sports? That kind of thing.'

So I told Mr Atapattu a little bit about school and Reach For The Top. And I told him that I like watching the GWF on TV.

'I watch the GWF, too,' he said, which surprised me. 'My favorite is the Exterminator.'

'The Exterminator? Are you kidding me?'

So we argued about the merits of the Exterminator versus the Great Dane for a while, and it was actually a really good discussion. Then suddenly, out of the blue, he said, 'Is everything OK at your place?'

'What do you mean?'

'I found you outside in the pouring rain in your socks. And you didn't want to buzz your father, even though he appears to be home.'

Oh. 'Everything's fine,' I said. 'Honest.'

As if on cue, my phone bleeped. It was a text from my dad: *Coast is clear.*

I put down my cup and reluctantly took off the Slanket. 'I have to go now. Thank you for the tea.' I headed for the door, passing a weird contraption sitting in a chair.

'What's that?'

'*Ten Second Abs.* Another Home Shopping Network purchase. Personally I find it too difficult. You are welcome to borrow it, if you like.' He said this without once looking at my wobblies.

'OK,' I said. 'Thanks.'

'You can come over anytime, Henry,' he told me as I

left, carrying the *Ten Second Abs* machine in one hand and my wet socks in the other. 'And keep the socks.'

'What's that?' Dad asked when I entered the apartment.

I didn't answer. I just put down the *Ten Second Abs* machine and waited for him to apologize.

He didn't. 'Am I getting the silent treatment?'

He was.

'Henry, she was just dropping off our mail.'

'Whatever. I never want to see her in our apartment again.'

'That's not up to you. For crying out loud, we just talked for a while.'

'Well, you seemed to be having an awfully good time.'

'Actually, I was. It was the first adult conversation I've had in a very long time.'

'You talk to Mom a few times a week.'

Dad looked away. 'Those conversations are different. They're very emotional, Henry.'

'Plus you work around adults every day.'

'Yeah, and aside from "Pass me the hammer" or "Work faster, Larsen," there's not a lot of chit-chat. Most of the guys don't even speak English.'

'She's trying to steal you away from Mom.'

He sighed. 'Henry. Nobody's going to "steal me away." But I think we have to be realistic here . . .'

'Realistic about what?'

There was a pause. 'Nothing.'

'No, say it.'

'Nothing. I'm going to start supper.' He turned and walked into the kitchen.

'She's coming back!' I shouted after him.

'Did I say she wasn't?' he hollered back.

'No, but you're thinking it!'

Now it was his turn not to answer.

7:00 a.m.

I've got a brilliant idea. And it is all thanks to Hayley Mills. She is the star of the original version of a movie called *The Parent Trap*.

I was having another sleepless night. Finally, at 4:00 a.m., I gave up trying to sleep and went into the living room. I started channel-surfing, and I came upon this movie.

Hayley Mills plays two characters – twins Sharon and Susan. Sharon and Susan spend most of the movie trying to get their divorced parents back together again. They even surprise them by reenacting their first date. And guess what? They *succeed*. It is a happy ending.

When the movie was over, I crawled back into bed. I was drifting off to sleep when it hit me: I can do the same thing. I can reunite my parents. I can't reenact their first date, but I *can* plan the best night ever.

I can take them to the *GWF Smash-Up Live!* in Seattle. Garbage-picking, here I come.

Tuesday, February 26

Recycling Managerial Services –
Rules to Live By

by Henry K. Larsen

1. Wear rubber gloves. Just because the recycling bins say CANS AND BOTTLES ONLY does not mean all students respect it.

At the very first bin we emptied at 7:30 this morning, I stuck my arm in practically up to my armpit and touched, not metal or glass, but something oozy and soft. When I lifted it out, I screamed like a girl. I was holding a half-eaten burger patty that was writhing with maggots. I won't mention what else Farley and I touched today, but let's just say it included three used snot rags, a cup full of congealed gravy, and a dead mouse. Which brings me to Rule #2.

2. Wear a layer of protective gear over your clothes.

That congealed gravy wasn't *that* congealed, and some of it splashed onto my shirt. Plus we discovered that kids throw a lot of half-finished sodas into the bins. Splash-back is inevitable.

3. *Keep a bar of soap, a towel, and a stick of deodorant in your locker.*

Recycling Managerial Services is surprisingly sweaty work. I had no supplies to freshen up with, and when I had to stand next to Alberta at our cooking station in Home Ec, she said, 'You stink.'

Rude.

4. *If you embark on a new entrepreneurial scheme that involves removing school property, it's a good idea to get permission first.*

Farley was rifling through the third bin (we took turns while the other person held open the garbage bag) when our vice principal, Mr Mackey, rounded the corner. 'What do you boys think you're doing?' he said.

'Oh, hey, Mr Mackey,' said Farley, without a hint of embarrassment. Then he proceeded to tell Mr Mackey *every last detail* about our plan to raise money for the *GWF Smash-Up Live!* in Seattle.

Mr Mackey thought it over. 'I guess it's alright, as long as you don't make a mess. And as long as you don't collect during school hours.'

'It's a deal, Sir!' said Farley. He tried to shake Mr Mackey's hand, but the VP took one look at Farley's filthy, sticky fingers and walked away.

5. Plan your route well.

We found ourselves near the boys' change room just before 8:30 – exactly the time team practices wrap up.

Farley's arm was deep in a bin, so he was looking the other way when Troy burst through the double doors from outside, his rugby uniform smeared with mud. He headed toward the change room, away from us. I breathed a sigh of relief – till Farley yelled, 'Gatorade Central! We've hit the mother lode!'

I was sure Troy would turn around. But luck was on our side. He just kept walking into the change room.

Still. It was a close encounter of a possibly nasty kind. We've agreed we need to map out a route that will achieve minimum exposure. Thursday we'll *start* near the change rooms.

6. Analyze your transportation needs before you begin.

We filled four garbage bags with cans and bottles this morning. It took a lot of maneuvering to cram them into our lockers. But after school, we faced the true challenge: how to lug the bags to the recycling depot, which is eight long blocks away.

First we had to wait for a good half hour for most of the kids to clear out. Then we tried carrying two bags each. We knew it was impossible before we reached the stairs. 'We'll have to do two trips,' Farley said.

But even carrying one bag each was hard work. The bottles were heavy and clunked against our shins. My bag almost split open. By the time we reached the recycling depot, we were pooped.

The depot was packed with people. Some of them showed up in Subaru Outbacks and Volvo station wagons; most people had shopping carts or baby buggies, piled high with cans and bottles.

We had to wait in line for over twenty minutes. The guy behind us started tapping me hard on the shoulder. I turned around. He smelled pretty ripe, and his hair was long and matted.

'Where'd you find all that loot?' he asked.

I guess I was overwhelmed, both by his smell and his mouthful of rotten teeth, because I didn't answer right away.

'You better not be taking any stuff between Broadway and 16th,' he said. 'Cos that's *my* turf.'

'We weren't near your turf,' Farley said, taking a step backward. 'Honest.'

'We got them from the recycling bins at our high school,' I told him.

He broke into a grin. 'Good thinking.' He extended a rough, dirty hand. 'Name's Preacher Paul. You ever need any advice, I'm your guy.'

We didn't want to be rude so we both shook his hand.

'First piece of advice,' he continued, even though we hadn't asked, 'get yourselves a buggy or a cart.'

He gave us other advice too as we inched forward in line. Things like, 'Remember, the government is watching you at all times,' and, 'Don't ever let them put a microchip in your brain.'

Finally we were able to sort our cans and bottles into cardboard flats. When we were done, we handed the flats to the guy behind the counter.

He punched some numbers into his register, opened it – and handed us eleven dollars and fifty cents.

Farley and I nodded good-bye to Preacher Paul and left the depot. We walked all the way back to the school, grabbed the last two bags, walked all the way back, and waited in line for another twenty minutes.

This time, the guy handed us twelve dollars and ten cents.

We left the depot again. We walked around the corner. Then we grabbed each other and jumped up and down. 'Twenty-three dollars and sixty cents!' Farley shouted. 'That's amazing!'

We took our money and headed to the big dollar store just east of Blenheim. We bought rubber gloves, heavy-duty garbage bags, a couple of chef's aprons, and some soap. That left us with exactly one dollar and seventeen cents.

Still. We were already into profits.

'*GWF Smash-Up Live!* here we come!' announced Farley.

'Um. I'd like to bring one more person, if that's OK.'

'Who?'

'My mom.'

'She's a GWF fan?'

'Huge.'

'So, they're not getting divorced.'

'Did I *ever* say they were getting divorced??'

'So where is she?'

'Away. On business.'

Farley just looked at me with his magnified eyes. I could tell he didn't believe me. But all he said was, 'One more ticket plus a little more spending money . . . We should probably raise another hundred bucks. That brings our grand total to five hundred.'

'I know it's not really fair, cos I'll be using three-quarters of the money—'

'So? I don't mind.' Then he opened his palm, revealing the loonie and change we had left. 'Check it out. Only four hundred and ninety-eight dollars and eighty-three cents to go!'

Maybe I don't need an upgrade, after all.

Thursday, February 28

After Farley and I did our rounds this morning (which went much smoother, thanks to our new rules), we lugged our garbage bags back to our lockers. Something was leaning against my locker door.

It was a baby stroller, covered in a thick layer of dust.

'There's a note,' Farley said.

I picked up the piece of paper and read it: '*For transporting you're garbadge. Alberta.*'

'Wow. Now I know why she never answers the spelling questions at Reach For The Top,' Farley said.

I thanked her later in Home Ec.

'No probs. I found it in our basement.'

'You're sure your parents won't mind?'

'Are you kidding? It's like an episode of *Hoarders* down there,' she said. 'Trust me, no one will notice it's gone.' We were at our cooking stations, making muffins.

The timer went off. I took my tray of apple cinnamon muffins out of the oven. They looked perfect – golden and delicious. Alberta took hers out. They were brown and burnt.

Mrs Bardus was doing her rounds. Just before she came to our station, Alberta said, 'Oh my God, look!' and pointed at something over my shoulder.

I turned around. 'What? I don't see anything.'

When I turned back, her tray of burnt muffins sat on the counter in front of me. '*Tsk, tsk,*' Mrs Bardus said, looming up behind us. 'I expected more from you, Henry. These look and feel like rocks. Completely inedible.' Then she turned to Alberta, who held *my muffins* in her oven-mitt-clad hands. Mrs Bardus plucked a muffin out of the tray and took a bite. 'Delicious!' she said with her mouth full. 'Nicely done, Alberta. This is a first.'

Mrs Bardus moved on to the next station. And Alberta burst out laughing. '*Ha-ha-ha-ha-ha-ha-HEEE-haw!*'

RUDE!!!

But guess what? The stroller is perfect. If we balance the bags really carefully, we can bring them all to the recycling depot in one go. Never mind that one of the wheels is wonky and makes the stroller veer to the left all the time – it's still a huge improvement.

Do other kids laugh when they see us pushing a baby stroller piled high with garbage bags? Yes. Do they laugh when they see us at school in our aprons and rubber gloves (cos no matter how early we get there, there are *always* a few kids who are there even earlier than us)? Of course they do. But when they find out how much money Farley and I have made in just one week, they laugh a lot less.

And, of course, my work doesn't stop with Recycling

Managerial Services. I'm also laying the groundwork for my plan.

Every time Mom and I talk, I make sure I'm always really chatty. She asks me to tell her all about school. So I do, in minute detail. I'm never, ever frosty with her. I tell her about the Reach For The Top team; I tell her about Farley and Alberta. I tell her about Mr Atapattu.

I do not tell her about Karen.

I tell her about the flowers that are already blooming in February and about the trees that have exploded with cherry blossoms, because I know that was one of her favorite things about living on the West Coast.

I do my best to paint a nice, happy picture of our lives out here.

And whenever she's missed one of the GWF shows, I tell her what happened in such vivid detail that she says, 'I feel like I'm there.'

And in the back of my head, I'm thinking, *You WILL be there! And sooner than you think!*

Saturday, March 2

Cecil is a jerk.

He started our session yesterday by talking about my behavior with Carol. 'You really frightened her, Henry. You told her you were going to shoot her.'

'I did not! I told her I was going to *zap* her. With my ray gun. Big, significant difference.' I unzipped my backpack and stuffed my hat inside.

'Still, you might consider apologizing.'

'*You* should apologize.'

'For what?'

'For subjecting me to such a horrible therapist! From now on, I speak to no one but you.'

He smiled. 'So, you *do* want to talk to me.'

'I don't *want* to. But if I *have* to talk to someone, I want it to be you.'

I swear he looked a little pleased, like I'd just paid him a compliment.

'I couldn't help but notice: you're carrying the journal I gave you.' He pointed at my backpack, which was still open on the floor. Sure enough, this book was poking up just enough for him to recognize it.

'So? I use it for homework.'

'Oh. OK.'

We sat in silence for at least a minute after that. I

think he was hoping I'd break down and start talking, but really, as if.

'What's new in your world?' he finally asked.

So I told him about Recycling Managerial Services. I told him that Farley and I had already made thirty-six dollars and twenty-nine cents, and that's *after* the money we spent on supplies. I told him that our goal is to bring in at least fifty bucks a week between now and the end of April, excluding March Break.

He was impressed. 'Holy Moly! You're a real entrepreneur, Henry. Are you saving up for anything special?'

'I most certainly am.'

'What?'

So I told him all about the *GWF Smash-Up Live!* in Seattle.

'Who's going with you?'

'My mom and dad.'

He paused. 'Your mom and dad?'

I nodded. 'They don't know it yet. It's a surprise.'

He pulled on his ponytail. 'Your mom's still in the hospital, Henry. In Ontario.'

'So? She won't be in there forever. It's still two months away.'

He pulled on his ponytail again. 'When tragedy occurs in a family . . . it can take a long time to heal. Sometimes, things never go back to the way they were before.'

'Duh,' I said. But I knew what he was driving at. He was trying to tell me my parents might *never* get back together. Cecil and my dad could start a Pessimists Society.

'I just don't want you to get your hopes up.'

I didn't answer.

He put his feet on the desk. This time his socks were pink and his left heel poked through. 'What are you thinking?'

'I'm Thinking. You Should Start Living. In the Twenty-First. Century. And Cut Off. That Gross. Ponytail,' I said in Robot-Voice.

Then I got up and left.

Screw Cecil.

Screw this journal.

I only wrote this entry so that I could make the following announcement: I quit.

Friday, March 8

OK, so I didn't quit. But I am only writing because I need to record what happened today.

First of all, I got to miss my session with Cecil (hallelujah!) because we had our seventh Reach For The Top game after school. It was at St Patrick's, a private school up the hill.

They crushed us.

'No worries, guys,' Mr Jankovich said to us as we packed up our gear. 'We're still going to the Provincials in Richmond in early April.'

'We've qualified for the Provincials?' I said. 'That's great!'

'*Any* team can go to the Provincials,' said Koula dismissively.

'Yes, but not *any* team has won five out of seven of their games so far,' Mr Jankovich replied.

When we left the school, I was totally surprised to see Dad in the parking lot, leaning against his truck, still in his work clothes and boots.

'You saw that?' I groaned.

But he was beaming. 'That was amazing! I had no idea you knew so much,' he said. Then he ruffled my hair in front of all of my teammates, which was embarrassing and nice at the same time. 'I think you knew about the cheese-rolling contest in Gloucestershire from *Uncle John's Bathroom Reader*, am I right?'

I smiled. 'Bingo.'

'Are you going to introduce me to your friends?'

He meant Farley and Alberta, who were hovering behind me. I was still mad at Alberta for the muffin switch, but I introduced them both anyway.

'Anyone want to grab a Blizzard at DQ?' Dad asked.

That threw me. *What if Dad starts talking about Jesse?* I thought. But I figured this was unlikely; even when it's just the two of us, he never talks about Jesse.

Farley and Alberta both said yes, and next thing I knew, we were all piling into the truck. Farley yelled, 'Shotgun!' which I thought was unfair since it was *my* dad's truck. But I didn't argue; I just squeezed into the cramped backseat with Alberta.

Farley talked my dad's ear off during the fifteen-minute drive. 'I hear you're a GWF fan,' he began, and I kicked the back of his seat hard because I was afraid he was going to ruin our surprise.

But he didn't. He just asked my dad who his favorite wrestler was (the Twister) and compared stats on the Twister (Height: five feet eleven, Weight: 265, Signature Move: Atomic Skull Crusher) to stats on Vlad the Impaler (Height: six feet four, Weight: 302, Signature Move: Human Torture Rack).

While they talked wrestling, Alberta tried to get my attention by poking me in the ribs. I ignored her at first. When I couldn't take it anymore, I blurted, 'Stop touching me.'

So she started waving her finger millimeters from my face instead. 'I'm not touching you. I'm not touching you.'

Jesse used to do that to me. It drove me mental. I'd wind up grabbing his hand and trying to bring him down with a Supersonic Arm Twist (the Exterminator's signature move), but he'd easily break free and pull me to the ground and tickle me till I'd almost pee my pants.

It would be impossible to put Alberta into a Supersonic Arm Twist in the back of the truck (and, if I'm honest, I think she'd easily take me in a fight), so I just turned away and stared out the window.

Farley was talking at full volume in the front seat, so I didn't hear Alberta unzip my backpack. That's not true – I heard her unzip *a* backpack, I just assumed it was *her* backpack. A moment later, she said, 'What's the *K* stand for?'

I turned. She was holding my journal, this very book, which I'd left in my backpack since my last session with Cecil. 'And why is your journal reluctant? How can a notebook be reluctant?' she asked.

I grabbed the journal from her hands. 'Quit snooping! That's private.'

'I didn't open it. As if I care what you write about.'

I shoved it back into my bag and clutched the pack to my chest.

After a moment, she said, 'Do you write about me in there?'

'Hardly,' I snorted, but I could feel my ears burn. 'Anyway, I thought you didn't care what I write about.'

'I don't.'

Alberta and I rode the rest of the way in silence. When we pulled into the Dairy Queen parking lot, I practically catapulted out of the truck.

We had a good time at DQ. Dad bought us all Blizzards. Farley got his with Smarties; Alberta and I both got cookie dough.

Farley left just before six because he'd promised Maria he'd be home for dinner. Then my dad went to the bathroom. And Alberta said, 'You're mad about the muffins.'

'Yes.'

'Kinda stupid, don't you think?'

'I lost marks, thanks to you.'

'Big dealio. It's Home Ec.'

'Well, if it isn't a *big dealio* to you, then don't do it again.'

'Whatever you say, Henry Kenneth Larsen.'

'Nice try.'

'Karl? Kerby? Kenilworth?'

'Not even close.'

'Look,' she said. 'I have an idea. Why don't you come over to my house this weekend and teach me how to bake? That way I'll never have to pull the ol' switcheroo again. Sunday, one o'clock?'

I almost choked on a chunk of cookie dough. 'I guess I could maybe do that.'

She took a pen out of her backpack, grabbed my hand, and wrote her address in my palm. Then my dad came back and asked Alberta if she'd like a ride home.

'Nah, thanks anyway. I just live a few blocks east of here.' She put on her coat; it was sheepskin and smelled like rotting animal flesh. 'Nice to meet you, Mr Larsen. Thanks a lot for the Blizzard.'

On the drive home, Dad said, 'Manitoba likes you.'

'Alberta. And she does not.'

But secretly I think maybe she does.

When we entered Cedar Manor, Karen and Mr Atapattu were in the foyer, screaming at each other.

'It is common courtesy to dispose of your junk mail!' he said.

'But I've posted a sign on my mailbox – NO JUNK MAIL! And they keep delivering junk mail! I shouldn't have to clean it up!'

'Then who *should* clean it up?'

'Whoever keeps delivering it!'

'And when do you think that will happen? When hell freezes over, perhaps?'

'Everything OK here?' my dad said.

Karen nodded. She was wearing tons of makeup, a miniskirt, and another pair of highly impractical shoes. 'Just this jerk,' she said, waving her hand toward Mr Atapattu. 'Nothing I can't handle.' A taxi pulled up out front. 'There's my cab.'

She tottered out the front door on her high heels, and as she passed me, I smelled a waft of perfume and booze.

'She is a horrible woman!' Mr Atapattu said when she was gone.

'She's not so bad,' said my dad.

'I'm with Mr Atapattu,' I said. 'She's gross.'

Since the elevator was still broken, the three of us walked up the stairs to the second floor together.

'And I am *not* a jerk,' Mr Atapattu muttered.

'Of course you aren't,' said my dad.

We arrived outside our door. 'I made a big pot of chicken curry this afternoon,' said Mr Atapattu. 'If you haven't already eaten, you would do me a great favor by sharing it with me.'

'I was going to order a pizza,' said my dad. 'Hockey game's about to start.' Mr Atapattu's face fell. Then Dad said, 'If you don't mind eating in front of the TV, you'd be welcome to join us.'

Mr Atapattu grinned. 'I would like that very much.'

And you know what? We had a pretty good evening.

And you know what else? I think his teeth *are* getting whiter.

Sunday, March 10

This was the best weekend of my life. And also the worst.

On Saturday morning, at about ten o'clock, our phone rang. I was still in bed, and I didn't try to answer it because I assumed it was a telemarketer. But then my dad hollered, 'Henry, it's for you.'

It was Farley. 'Wanna come over and play video games?' he said.

So, for the first time since we moved here, I went to a friend's house. I think Dad was pretty pleased because his eyes got all watery and he said, 'Stay as long as you like. I'll do the grocery shopping.'

I left after breakfast. Two new signs were posted in the foyer. The first said PLEASE KEEP COMMON AREAS TIDY AND RECYCLE YOUR JUNK MAIL. The second said WHAT IS THIS, A DICTATORSHIP???

I walked up to Farley's place. He lives on 15th Ave, about six blocks straight up the hill. My jaw almost dropped when I arrived outside his house. It's *huge* – flesh-colored stucco with actual columns out front.

Farley was at the window, watching for me. He ran to the front door and flung it open. 'Hi! Welcome! Enter!'

He took me on a tour of the place. This took awhile because his house is at least five times the size of our apartment. It was weird, though. Only a few of the rooms were furnished: Farley's bedroom, one of the guest rooms (for Maria), the family room, and the kitchen. All the other rooms were empty. It felt kind of like a ghost town.

Maria was in the kitchen, putting on her coat. 'You be a good boy,' she said to Farley, patting him on the cheek. Then she left.

'Saturday's the day she visits her sister in Surrey,' Farley explained. 'But she left snacks.'

We set ourselves up in the family room and played on Farley's PS3 for hours. Then we went to the local park and threw a Frisbee around. When we came back, we played more video games. Finally, at around five, I told him I should go. Maria still wasn't back.

'She stays out there for supper and takes the last bus home,' he told me. 'It's OK, I have money to order a pizza. And *Saturday Night Smash-Up* is on later.'

I suddenly felt really sad for Farley, which was almost refreshing after so many months of only feeling sad for myself. 'You could come to our place,' I said. 'We're going to order pizza, too.'

He grinned. 'Really?'

So Farley came over, and the three of us ordered pizza and watched *Saturday Night Smash-Up* together. When the Great Dane gave Vlad the Impaler his signature Body Splash, I cheered and Farley booed. It was fun.

Dad and I gave Farley a ride home afterward. All the lights were off; Maria still wasn't back.

'It's OK,' he said. 'She'll be home by midnight.' We waited till he was safely inside. He looked dwarfed by that huge, empty house.

Later, after I'd brushed my teeth, I gave Dad a hug.

'What's that for?' he said, hugging me back.

'Nothing.' I didn't feel like explaining that for the first time since IT happened, I actually felt lucky to have at least *one* parent to go home to.

Sunday morning went on forever. Dad could tell I was nervous because I changed my shirt five times (I finally settled on light gray) and my pants twice. I went with the cargo pants. They were loose; I had to borrow a belt from Dad. Maybe all the bottle-collecting and *Ten Second Abs* work is starting to pay off.

Finally, at 12:15, I couldn't take it any longer. I had to leave.

'Have fun with Ontario,' Dad said.

'Alberta!' I shouted as I closed the door.

Alberta lives east and south of me by ten blocks, on the other side of the school. It took me only fifteen minutes to get there, so I had to walk around the block over and over again.

From the outside, her house is the opposite of Farley's. It's small and made of wood, and it's painted in a color I can only describe as *neon yellow*. It looks like it might collapse at any moment.

The grass looks like it hasn't been cut in a year. Toys, scooters, and rusted lawn furniture litter the lawn and the sagging porch.

At exactly one o'clock – after six turns around the block – I rang the bell. A girl answered it almost immediately. She was an older, taller, skinnier version of Alberta, minus the lazy eye and the unique fashion sense. She wore a soccer uniform covered in grass stains, like she'd just come home from a game.

'You must be Alberta's little friend,' she said, and I swear she emphasized the word *little*.

'And you must be Cricket,' I replied.

'Cricket, I *said* I'd get it!' Alberta shouted, taking the stairs two at a time. She was wearing pajama bottoms, which were white with black sheep all over them, and a T-shirt that read *Does Not Play Well with Others*. She tried to shove her older sister out of the way, but Cricket just planted her arms against the door frame and wouldn't budge.

'Was that you I saw walking past our house over and over again?' Cricket said. 'Are you *stalking* us?'

I begged my face not to go red. I don't think it listened. 'I was early,' I said, and my voice cracked.

'Get lost, Cricket! Get a life!'

Cricket just shrugged. 'Behave,' she said as she finally stepped out of the doorway and headed up the stairs.

Alberta pulled me inside. 'I *hate* her!' she said.

I used to say that about Jesse, too. 'You don't really hate her,' I replied. 'You just don't like what she does to you sometimes.'

'No. I hate her,' she said. 'C'mon, let's go to the kitchen.'

The inside of their house was just as messy as the outside. In fact, it wasn't just messy; it was filthy. Food-encrusted dishes were piled high in the sink; newspapers, books, homework, bills, and at least three separate pairs of sweaty socks covered the tables, chairs, and countertops. Dust bunnies and crumbs were all over the floor. Dad and I aren't the best housekeepers, but compared to Alberta's, our place is spotless.

'Where are your parents?'

'Mom's working. She's a nurse's aide at an old folks' home. And Dad's probably in the garage with Dylan. They're building a boxcar for some big race in the spring.'

'Who's Dylan?'

'My little brother.'

'I didn't know you had a brother.'

'He's eight. Him, I like.'

I'd brought over a recipe I'd found on Epicurious for banana chocolate-chip muffins. We got to work. And even though Cricket kept wandering through and saying things like, 'I want you kids to keep six inches between you at all times,' and even though Dylan came running into the kitchen and knocked our bowl of freshly made batter onto the filthy floor, and even though I almost hurled when Alberta bent down and *scooped it back into the bowl*, it was a great afternoon. Her mom came home just as the muffins were cooling, and everyone, even Cricket, tried one. They were delicious, in spite of the odd hair.

'Nice work, dear,' her mom said, then she gave Alberta a big hug. Alberta said, 'Mom!' but I could tell she loved it. I kind of wished her mom would hug me, too.

Then her parents went out to do the grocery shopping, and Dylan went into the living room to watch a DVD. Alberta packed up a few muffins for me to bring home.

'Thanks for helping me today, Henry,' she said as she handed me my muffins. Then she kissed me.

Yes, that's right: she kissed me. Not on the cheek. On the lips. Her lips were soft, like little pillows.

I kissed her back. I didn't close my eyes like I was probably supposed to. I stared at her, kissing me.

'*Woot! Woot!* Six-inch rule violated! Six-inch rule violated! Sound the alarm! *Woot! Woot!*' Cricket. You could tell she was having the time of her life.

'Get lost!' Alberta shouted. She chased her sister around the kitchen, trying to hit her with a wet dish towel. Cricket just laughed and laughed. Then her cell phone rang, and she left the room to answer it.

'You won't *believe* what I just caught my little sister doing,' we could hear her saying. 'She's such a slut!'

'*Aaaagh!!!* I hate her so much,' Alberta said. 'I wish she was dead!'

'No, you don't.'

'Yes, I do. Life would be *so much better!*'

'No. It wouldn't.'

I think my voice sounded weird. Cos suddenly she was looking at me, with both eyes.

'How do you know?'

I shrugged. 'I just think you should be careful about saying stuff like that. Because if it came true, you'd hate yourself forever.'

She took my hand. 'Are you talking from personal experience?'

I don't know if it was our kiss, or the concern in her voice, or the feel of her surprisingly rough hand over mine, but I said, 'I had a brother.'

'Did he die?'

I nodded.

'Crap, Henry. I don't know what to say. I'm really sorry. How'd he die?'

The lie came easily. 'Cancer.'

'What kind?'

146

'The deadly kind.'

'No, but where?'

'. . . The brain.'

'A tumor?'

'Yes.'

'How long ago?'

'Last June.' That part was true.

'Is that why your mom doesn't live with you?' She saw the look on my face. 'Farley told me.'

'She's in Ontario. But she's moving back with us soon. She just needed some time to clear her head.'

'Oh.'

'Please don't tell anyone,' I said. 'Especially not Farley. No one else knows. I'd like to keep it that way.'

Alberta nodded. Then she kissed me again.

And her sister didn't interrupt this time.

When I got home, I went to my room and replayed the kiss over and over in my head. I was *so happy*. And then suddenly it hit me like a punch to the stomach: Jesse would never, ever feel a girl's lips on his. He would never get to feel his first boobs; he would never get to go to college, or catch another fish, or travel, or have kids.

He would never experience anything, ever again. And neither would Scott.

And I felt *so sad* for both of them, but especially for

my brother, which I know isn't right, but it's true because he was *my brother*. And then, *boom*, like that, my sadness turned to furies because it dawned on me that *every single time* something GOOD happens to me, Jesse will be there, looming over my shoulder, like a big inescapable force of doom, *for the rest of my life*.

~~*I only did what you told me to do!* I wanted to shout at him. *It is not my fault! You told me not to tell anyone what happened in the park on April 30! You made me promise!*~~

2:00 a.m.
Sometimes I wish Jesse was alive again, just so I could kill him.

Monday, March 11

6:00 a.m.

I just had the craziest dream.

I'm in the ring on *Saturday Night Smash-Up*. I'm wearing an outfit that looks a lot like the Great Dane's. I'm taller and more muscular than in real life. My wobblies are gone.

They announce my opponent. It's Vlad the Impaler. Vlad steps into the ring. Except it isn't Vlad. He's wearing Vlad's costume, including the little black mask that covers the top half of his face. But I recognize the eyes peering out at me. They're Jesse's.

The fight begins. Vlad is no match for me. I use every dirty trick in the book, including eye pokes, biting, and low blows. Vlad barely fights back.

It ends when I whack him repeatedly in the head with a metal chair. He crumples onto the mat and lies there, unmoving.

The ref holds up my arm, and I dance around the ring to the cheers of the crowd.

But above the roar of the crowd, I hear a sound: duct tape, being torn off a roll. The ref isn't holding up my arm anymore. He's leaning over Jesse, putting a pillowcase over his head. Then the ref looks up and smiles at me. It's Scott Marlin.

That's when I woke up, panting and drenched in sweat.

Tuesday, March 12

Progress. Serious progress.

I was in the middle of doing some ab crunches with the *Ten Second Abs* thing when Mom called.

I took the phone into my room. We had a long talk. After I'd told her about going to Farley's house and baking muffins with Alberta (minus the kiss) and about the best fights on *Saturday Night Smash-Up*, she said, 'I have some good news.'

'What?'

'I'm not in the hospital anymore. Dr Dumas and I agreed I was ready to come home.'

My heart did a flip. 'Home?'

'To Pop-Pop and Grams's,' she said. 'I still need to see Dr Dumas a few times a week, as an outpatient.'

'Oh.'

'I'd really like to see you at March Break.'

'March Break is next week.'

'I know.'

My knees felt weak, and I had to sit down. 'I'd like to see you, too,' I said. Understatement of the year. 'When are you coming out?'

'Actually,' she said, 'I was hoping you'd come here.'

'Why?'

'Pop-Pop and Grams have offered to fly you out on air miles. They have enough points.'

'But if they have enough points for me to fly there, they have enough for you to fly here.'

There was a pause. 'I don't want to miss my sessions with Dr Dumas. Will you consider it? Please? I really want to see you.'

There was nothing to consider. 'I'll come,' I said.

'Oh, hooray!' she replied. Written down it looks insincere, but when she said it, it was genuine.

When I got off the phone, I went back into the living room. Dad was watching TV. I told him what Mom had said. 'You can come, too. We can convince her to fly back out with us.'

Dad got this funny look on his face. 'I think your mom wants some one-on-one time with you, Henry.'

'But she wants to see you, too.'

'Did she say that?'

'No, but I'm sure she's thinking it.'

Dad sighed. 'I can't take the time, anyway. I'm in the middle of this big construction job . . .'

'So. Ask for a week off.'

'I can't afford to take a week off, Henry. You know that.'

I could tell from his tone that it was time to drop it.

So the situation isn't perfect. But it's pretty darn close. And it will be much easier to convince her, face-to-face, that it's time to be a family again.

Friday, March 15

INTRIGUING FACT: On December 17, 1903, the Wright brothers flew one of their planes for twelve seconds straight. It was the first successful powered piloted flight in history.

And now, here I am, over a century later, flying four hours to Toronto. That's twelve seconds times I don't know how much, but it's a lot. After that, I'll take another, smaller plane to Kingston, where Pop-Pop will pick me up.

This is my fifth trip on a plane. The first two times, we flew to Pop-Pop and Grams's. The third time, we flew to San Diego and Legoland. The fourth time, we flew to Pop-Pop and Grams's to live with them after IT.

That was an awful trip. Mom was so sedated that she slurred her words, and some of the passengers thought she was drunk. Dad was quiet, but every now and then he'd let loose with these huge, quavering sighs. I sat in between them, and it was the longest four hours of my life. Jesse wasn't with us; he'd been left behind in a storage locker. I guess that sounds awful, but we could hardly put him in our luggage. And imagine the questions from the security staff if we'd tried to take him as carry-on.

But enough of that. I refuse to let bad memories spoil this trip. *This* trip is going to be fun. I am going for a whole week, Friday to Friday. Those were the dates Pop-Pop could get with his air miles.

Best part of a Friday-to-Friday trip: I get to miss two, count 'em, two, sessions with Cecil!!!

I have a window seat, and it's a clear day. I'm staring down at the Rocky Mountains, and they are spectacular. A guy in a business suit is in the aisle seat, and the middle seat is empty. I've already watched a movie that my parents wouldn't let me see when it came out because they thought it was 'inappropriate'. And Pop-Pop made sure he bought me a meal voucher, which I spent on five mini-cans of Pringles.

Mountains to my left. Pringles to my right. My own personal TV.

This is the life.

Yesterday morning, Farley and I collected our biggest haul yet. But we had a Reach For The Top tournament after school, so we agreed to store the cans and bottles in our lockers and return them on the Monday after March Break.

Word has spread about our business, and mostly the response is good. A bunch of kids actually hand us their empty cans and bottles when they see us at our lockers, which saves us a bit of work.

Troy finally figured out what we're up to. I guess it had to happen, since his locker is right across the hall from ours. He makes fun of us. But yesterday, when he started talking about 'Fatty and Fartley's garbage-picking operation,' Farley said, 'Laugh all you want, Troy. We've made almost a hundred and fifty bucks in three weeks!'

That shut him up.

11:05 a.m. PST/2:05 p.m. EST
The flight attendant just gave me some extra little bags of pretzels. How cool is that?

11:45 a.m. PST/2:45 p.m. EST
The guy in the aisle seat has fallen asleep. He has just the tiniest bit of drool coming out of his mouth.

12:30 p.m. PST/3:30 p.m. EST
Also. I had a little talk with Dad before I left. I said, 'Don't even think of inviting Karen into our apartment.'

Dad sighed. He was in the galley kitchen making supper, wearing the John Deere apron Mom had made him for his birthday a few years ago. I was setting the table. 'Henry. I hardly know her. I'd barely even call her a friend, but she's certainly nothing more.'

'That's what *you* think,' I replied, 'but what does *she* think?'

'How would I know?' He served up scrambled eggs and toast onto two plates. We're trying hard to make our own meals these days, to save money and eat better, but until Mrs Bardus teaches me more than just baking in Home Ec, our list of recipes is short.

'Remember two summers ago?' I said. 'When we rented that cabin for a week?'

'Of course I remember. The fishing was great. Jesse caught that sockeye—' Dad stopped suddenly. He'd just broken our unwritten rule: never say Jesse's name out loud.

'And you could borrow movies from the front desk,' I reminded him. 'Most of them were really old. And we watched one called *Fatal Attraction*.'

'So?'

'So? How do you know Karen isn't like the crazy lady in that?' In the movie, a businessman is happily married with a wife and a kid, but he has a weekend fling with this woman who turns out to be a psycho. She stalks him *and* his family. One day, the family comes home to find a pot of water boiling on the stove. When they take off the lid, do you know what's inside?

Their daughter's rabbit!!!

'At least you don't have a pet,' my dad replied.

'Ha-ha. I'm serious, Dad. She's lonely, she's desperate, and she's after you. And *you're taken*.'

Dad put down his knife and fork and looked me in the eye. I thought he was going to lecture me, but instead he just said, 'Henry, you have my word. I will not let

Karen into our apartment while you're away.'

'Thank you,' I said. Then, just so he didn't think I was completely unreasonable, 'But feel free to invite Mr Atapattu over anytime.'

1:00 p.m. PST/4:00 p.m. EST

We land in just under an hour. The flight attendant just brought me another can of Coke. And I didn't even ask!

9:00 p.m. PST/12 Midnight EST

I'm in my room at Pop-Pop and Grams's. It's their guest room, and it's in the attic. It has sloped ceilings and hard-wood floors and a tiny window. If I stand on my tiptoes, I can see outside. It's cozy. I like it.

I had a nice surprise when I landed at the airport: Mom was there to meet me. She'd had a session with Dr Dumas in Kingston, so she stayed in town till my flight came in. She hugged me like she would never let me go. There were waterworks, and not just hers.

I cried because I was remembering how things used to be, before Jesse went and screwed it all up. And I cried because Mom doesn't look great. She's lost more weight than I've gained since June 1st. She has dark circles under her eyes. And I couldn't help but notice that her hair looks thinner. Worse, when she leaned down to pick up my duffel bag, I saw a bald spot.

On the way home in Pop-Pop's old Ford Escort, she kept stroking my arm and touching my face. 'Henry. My Henry,' she said over and over. It wasn't as creepy as it sounds. In fact, she was in a pretty good mood. 'I always feel better after one of my sessions,' she said.

It was dark on the drive home. She took Highway 33, which meant we got to take the Glenora Ferry, which is only my favorite ferry in the whole wide world. It takes just ten minutes to cross the bay, but it makes you feel like you're going somewhere special – to an island or something, even though it's really just an extension of the highway.

Pop-Pop and Grams were super-happy to see me. For dinner, Grams had made my favorite: roast beef. Halfway through the meal, Pop-Pop farted. Loudly.

I looked at my mom. She looked at me. And we both started to laugh. We laughed so hard, we couldn't stop. We laughed till tears were running down our faces.

It was an awesome moment.

It was just like old times.

Saturday, March 16

I slept for ten hours straight. I fell asleep at 1:00 a.m. (Picton time), and didn't wake up till 11:00 a.m. (Picton time).

For the first time in months, I had no nightmares. For the first time in months, I slept through the night.

Tuesday, March 19

Four days in, three days to go. All things considered, things are going surprisingly well, so *in your face, Cecil!* Mom may not look the greatest, but in other ways she seems a lot better than she did when we left at the end of December.

We have a routine to our days. Mom waits to have breakfast with me (even if I don't get up till eleven, which has happened every day so far), and she cooks me whatever I want: pancakes, waffles, bacon and eggs, anything. She doesn't eat much herself, although this morning she had two whole pancakes.

Then we go for a long walk, bundling up because there's still snow on the ground and you can see your breath. Mom asks me a lot of questions. She wants to know everything, down to the last detail.

'Main physical characteristic of each of your teachers,' she said yesterday.

'Mr Coulter, Phys Ed: no neck. Ms Wrightson, Math: talks like a ventriloquist's dummy. Mr Jankovich, Socials: wears socks with sandals. Mrs Bardus, Home Ec: stone-faced. Mr Schell, English: big ears.'

'Three words you'd use to describe your friend Farley. Quick, without thinking too much.'

'Weird. Enthusiastic. Loyal.'

'And Alberta?'

'Rude. Bold. Unique. Pretty.'

Mom smiled. 'That's four words.'

On Monday, she drove into Kingston for her session with Dr Dumas, so I stayed with Pop-Pop and Grams. Grams and I played Rummoli all afternoon. Today, the four of us drove to Sandbanks Provincial Park. It was a milder day, and we walked over the dunes and along the beach for over an hour.

Most afternoons, Mom and I pull out one of Pop-Pop and Grams's board games and play in the living room. That's when we discuss the person Dad and I never talk about at home.

Jesse. Mom talks about Jesse a lot.

One day she said, 'Remember when Jesse was four, he put the plastic cheese from Mouse Trap up his nose? And I had to take him to Emergency to get it removed?'

I didn't remember because I was only two at the time, but I'd heard the story a million times so I said, 'Yes.'

Another day she said, 'Remember the camping trip we took, near Tofino? And Dad bought you and Jesse a kite?'

I remembered. It was a beautiful kite, rainbow-colored and shaped like a dragon.

'Jesse loved that kite,' she said, gazing past me out the window. 'He'd fly that thing for hours every day.'

I loved that kite too. I flew it for hours every day, too, I thought. But all I said was, 'Yeah, he did.'

Today she said, 'Remember when Jesse was in second grade, he did that comedy routine for the talent show?' She chuckled. 'He stood up onstage and told knock-knock jokes for five minutes straight.'

'That was me,' I said.

'Pardon?'

'That was me,' I repeated. 'Not Jesse.'

Her smile faded. 'You're sure?'

I nodded. 'Knock-knock, who's there? Isaac. Isaac who? Isaac coming in! Remember?'

She chuckled, kind of. Fifteen minutes later, she murmured, 'I was sure that was Jesse.'

She never talks about what he did. In fact, she never talks about the last two years of his life. It's like she's frozen him in time at the age of twelve.

But mostly I think talking about Jesse is a good sign. She isn't bottling it all up, which I guess is what Dad and I do.

Speaking of Dad. If only I could get her to talk about *him*. It seems like every time I bring him up, she changes the subject.

Maybe I'm just imagining things.

Another good sign: Mom has asked me to come to her session with Dr Dumas tomorrow. She says he wants to meet me. I'd like to meet him, too. I want to tell him thanks for everything he's done and all that, but it's time for my mom to come home.

One thing.

One thing.

One thing.

3:00 p.m. EST/12:00 p.m. PST

When Cecil gave me this notebook, he told me that if I was having a lousy day – *especially* if I was having a lousy day – I should always try to write *one thing* in my journal.

For once, I took his advice.

4:00 p.m. EST/1:00 p.m. PST

I'm on the plane. Heading home. Alone.

Things did not go as planned.

Wednesday started well. Mom and I drove to Kingston at around ten in the morning. She'd washed her hair and put on a clean sweater, and I think she was even wearing a bit of makeup. It was a beautiful day – clear blue skies and a fresh dusting of snow. We took the Glenora Ferry again, which dropped us in Adolphustown, which does not deserve to be called a town. It should be called Adolphus*hamlet*.

The countryside is pretty. Not better than BC, just different. We drove through Bath, and I couldn't help thinking that if Jesse was with us, I would have said, *And boy do you need one!*

As we neared Kingston, we drove past the Collins Bay Institution. Weird as it sounds, I love that prison. I remember, on one of our visits to Pop-Pop and Grams when Jesse was still alive, the two of us gaped at the huge stone fortress with its towering red roof from the backseat of the car, and Jesse said, 'I want to live there.'

And all the adults laughed and laughed, and Grams said, 'Well, kiddo, let's hope you never, ever have to!'

Which is kind of funny when you think about it because if he'd survived, he would have wound up living in a prison.

Our first few hours in Kingston were great. Mom took me to Cooke's Fine Foods and Coffee, which is only my favorite store. It's been around since the olden days. It's dark and big, with high ceilings and wood floors, and it smells delicious. Mom bought me a piece of Brighton Rock.

Then we had lunch at Chez Piggy, which not only has the best name ever, it has the best food ever. We talked a lot, and Mom even joked with our waiter. For one brief hour, it was almost like IT had never happened.

Then we went to Dr Dumbass's office.

That is my new name for Dr Dumas. This guy makes Cecil look like a genius.

Dr Dumbass works out of the hospital with a few other psychiatrists, so we sat in a waiting room with a handful of people who looked completely mental. One guy, with long scraggly hair, kept talking to himself and laughing quietly, and there was an old woman with no teeth, who just stared into space. I'm pretty sure she was seriously medicated. Compared to them, my mom looked *one hundred per cent* normal!! No wonder I felt so optimistic.

Then Mom went into Dr Dumbass's office for her

appointment. The idea was that she would come and get me for the last fifteen minutes, so I'd have a chance to meet him. For forty-five minutes, I had to sit there pretending to read three-year-old issues of *Better Homes and Gardens* and *Reader's Digest* (YAWN), while the guy with long scraggly hair kept staring at me and laughing, which gave me the creeps.

Finally the door to Dr Dumbass's office opened, and he stepped out. He's super-tall – like, six feet six inches – skinny, with blond, thinning hair. He has a face that reveals nothing, which is probably good if you're a psychiatrist, but equally good if you're a serial killer.

Anyway, he smiled at me with his lips only and shook my hand. Dad thinks you can tell a lot about a man's character by the way he shakes hands. Dr Dumbass's handshake was limp.

'You must be Henry,' he said. I glanced at the other two nutbars in the waiting room and thought, *No shit, Sherlock*. 'Come on in.'

I followed him into his office. It was much bigger and cleaner and tidier than Cecil's office. He had a lot of framed degrees hanging on his wall. Mom sat in one of two armchairs across from his desk. I plopped into the other one. 'Your mother talks about you a lot,' he said.

Then he tried to ask me how I was coping, and I said, 'Fine.'

And he said, 'This is a safe place, Henry. You can talk openly about your feelings.'

And I said, 'I have my own doctor to do that with, thanks.'

'Well, what would you like to talk about?' he asked.

'My mom seems to be doing really well,' I said.

He smiled at my mom. 'She is indeed.'

'I think it's time for her to come home.' I turned to my mom. 'You could fly home with me this Friday. Or, if that's too soon, you could come out next week.'

The room went dead quiet. Mom and Dr Dumbass shared a look.

'Henry,' the doctor started, 'your mom is making great progress—'

'Yes, and we have you to thank.'

'But I feel it's in her best interest to continue her sessions with me for a while longer.'

I turned to Mom and placed her hand in mine. 'Well, it's not really up to you, is it?' I said to Dr Dumbass.

Mom looked down at my hand. 'Henry, you know how much I love you . . .'

'Which is why you need to come home.'

'Which is why I can't. Not yet.'

This wasn't how I'd rehearsed it in my head. 'C'mon, Mom. This whole nervous breakdown thing is getting a little old.'

Dead silence. 'A little old?' Dr Dumbass said. 'That implies some form of intention on your mother's part.'

I had no idea what he was talking about. 'There are good doctors in Vancouver, too,' I told Mom. 'You could see my psychologist, Cecil. He's no rocket scientist, but he's OK.'

'You don't understand,' Mom said. 'I'm not ready. I've already let one child down . . .'

'You didn't let Jesse down! What Jesse did was not your fault.' I looked at Dr Dumbass. 'You've told her what happened isn't her fault, right?'

'Yes. But your mother needs to get to that place on her own, Henry. And we've been making great strides, but we're not there yet.'

'Mom, please. You can't blame yourself.'

'But I do. And I need to be able to forgive myself.' She paused for a moment. 'I need to be able to forgive your father.'

I didn't like where this was headed *at all*. 'It wasn't his fault, either.'

'It was his gun. I told him I didn't want any kind of weapon in the house, I told him to get rid of it—'

'He couldn't know. He stored it properly, even the police said so.'

'We had a child in crisis. There should not have been a gun in the house.' She was getting angry now.

'That's so stupid—'

'Now, Henry, no feelings are stupid,' said Dr Dumbass, totally interrupting me.

I just kept my eyes on my mom. 'If you need to blame someone, blame Jesse! You can't blame Dad. He loves you. You love him. We need you with us. We miss you like crazy!'

'But don't you see, Henry, I'm not *me*, I'm a wreck—'

'So?? I'd rather have a wreck of a mother than no mother at all!'

There was a pause. I thought I'd finally gotten through to her. Then she said, 'I'm sorry. I'm just not ready.'

I felt like I'd been hit by a truck. 'You never would have done this to Jesse,' I said.

'What do you mean?'

'If it had been me instead of him. You *never* would have deserted Jesse.'

'That's unfair.'

'He was always your favorite. He's *still* your favorite, even though he's dead, even though he screwed up our lives forever!' I was shouting really loud by now. 'All I've ever done is be normal, and this is the thanks I get.'

'Henry,' my mom said. She started to cry.

Dr Dumbass was licking his lips, like he was actually excited. 'No, no, this is good, Francine. He's owning his feelings—'

My furies exploded. I leaped out of my chair and put my hands on his desk. I got inches from his stupid serial-killer face. 'Shut the hell up!!'

He wheeled his chair back against the wall. 'Henry, you need to take a deep breath.'

That's when I started talking Robot.

'Dr Dumbass. You. Are a Moron,' I said in my mono-tone voice.

'The name is Dumas.'

'Dumbass. Dumbass. Dumbass.' Then I turned to Mom. 'Mother-bot. You. Are Pathetic. I Hate You. And I Hate Jesse. You Can Both. Go to Hell. Oh, Wait. Jesse Is Probably. Already There.'

Then I robot-walked out of Dr Dumbass's office. The scraggly-haired guy was still in the waiting room, and he laughed when he saw me.

'Stop Laughing. You Freak,' I said to him in Robot. 'Freak. Crazy Man. Loon.'

It worked. He stopped laughing. He put his hands up to his face like he thought I was going to hit him, and you know what? For a split second, it gave me a total rush.

Then the rush vanished, and I felt like a total scumbag.

'I. Am Sorry,' I said to the crazy guy in Robot. 'Truly. Sorry.'

Then I robot-walked out of the hospital.

● ● ●

Mom and I drove home in silence. She cried the whole way, which made me want to hit her. *Get over yourself,* I wanted to scream. *You think you're the only one who's suffering??*

But I was done. My furies were gone. I just pressed my cheek against the cold window and closed my eyes.

I spent Thursday in my room. Grams brought me food on a tray and left it outside my door. Today Pop-Pop drove me to the airport. Mom didn't come.

Pop-Pop tried to talk to me, but I was just way too tired to answer.

'She loves you, Henry. More than anything,' he said as we stood outside the security gate.

I wouldn't make eye contact. I hoisted my backpack onto my shoulders and turned to get into the security lineup.

'Aren't you going to give your Pop-Pop a hug?'

No. I wasn't.

Just before I disappeared behind the frosted glass, I turned back and saw that Pop-Pop was crying.

My stomach churns when I think about that. But Pop-Pop and Grams aren't innocent. They are accessories to this crime. I've read about cases where people seek asylum in a church, like illegal immigrants or refugees who are about to be deported back to their home country.

They hide in a house of worship cos no one can make them leave. Well, Pop-Pop and Grams are like the church. They are harboring my mother.

And it's not fair because Dad and I are her rightful country.

5:00 p.m. EST/2:00 p.m. PST

This flight sucks. My TV is broken. And I'm stuck in a middle seat between two fatties. I know I still have some of my own wobblies, but I look like a stick compared to these two. One of them keeps trying to see what I'm writing. The fatties are traveling together, but do you think they'd sit beside each other and let me have the window or the aisle? No. They're forcing me to stay in the middle, where I am trapped in a sea of roly-poly arms and massive jiggling thighs that spill over into my space.

I think Window Fatty saw what I wrote. She's no longer trying to look over my shoulder, and she looks like she might cry.

As Alberta would say, *Whatevs*.

11:00 p.m.

Dad met me at the airport. He gave me a bear hug. 'The apartment's been way too quiet without you,' he said without letting go, and I could tell he was really happy I was back.

~~At least one parent loves me~~.

We didn't talk much in the car. He didn't ask me how the trip had gone or how Mom was, and that's when I realized he already knew. He'd already spoken to Mom, and probably to Pop-Pop and Grams, too. He'd heard the gory details.

'You're still in time for your appointment with Cecil,' he said as we neared Kitsilano. 'I called him. He said he'd love to see you.'

I surprised myself because I said, 'OK.'

I told Cecil everything about my visit. I confess I cried a bit, too. He just listened. He may not be a great psychologist, but he's a great listener.

Sitting in his dinky little office with the crappy furniture and the disgusting carpet, I realized something: I'd missed it. I'd missed Cecil.

And the best part about our session: even though he'd tried to warn me that my trip might not go as planned? He never once said *I told you so*.

Dad waited outside in his truck for my entire hour-long session, just so he could drive me home. We parked at the back of the building, by the garbage and recycling bins. New signs were posted above them. I recognized the handwriting. The first one said PLEASE, DO A BETTER JOB OF SEPARATING YOUR GLASS AND PLASTIC CONTAINERS.

The second one said PLEASE, QUIT BEING SO ANAL!!

'Mr Atapattu dropped off a container of chicken curry for us this morning,' Dad told me as we entered the apartment. 'He knew you were coming home tonight.'

Dad steamed some rice to go with it, and we ate in front of the TV.

'I love you, Dad,' I said, not taking my eyes off the screen.

'I love you, too, Henry.' He ruffled the top of my head. His eyes looked moist. But I think it was just the spices from the curry.

Tuesday, March 26

INTRIGUING FACT: Fruit flies reproduce like crazy. A female can lay hundreds of eggs at a time. They're attracted to anything sweet and sticky.

Why am I writing this?

Stay tuned.

Farley met me outside the school yesterday morning. Before I could stop him, he threw his arms around me. 'Welcome back!' He talked a mile a minute as we headed into the school and up the stairs to our lockers. 'March Break was *so boring*. Oh, and Alberta's home sick with the flu. She told me on Facebook to tell you. She also told me to tell you to get out of the Dark Ages and join Facebook. How was your week?'

I was spared having to answer that because, as we neared our lockers, we could see right away that we had a problem on our hands.

Clouds of teensy little bugs were flying in and out of the slats in our locker doors.

It got ten times worse when we opened them. Horror movie worse. *Thousands* of fruit flies flew out.

We slammed our locker doors shut. 'It's OK,' Farley said. 'We'll just bring the bags to the depot after school. The bugs will be gone by tomorrow.'

Famous last words.

• • •

After school, we took the bags to the depot.

By the time we arrived, there were only a few flies left; the cold air must have killed them. We thought our problems were solved. But this morning, after we'd done our rounds and lugged the fresh bags to our lockers, it was obvious that we were wrong. The fruit flies weren't gone; if anything, they'd multiplied. Talia, a tenth grader whose locker is between mine and Farley's, was disgusted. 'Get those things out of here!' she wailed, and on 'here', a fruit fly flew into her mouth. '*Aaagh*, I'm gonna barf!!' She bolted down the hall and into the girls' washroom. I never did find out if she actually barfed.

'If she tells the principal, our entire operation will be shut down,' Farley said.

I nodded. 'We need to deal with this. Pronto.'

First we lugged our fresh bags full of recyclables to Mr Jankovich's classroom and pleaded with him to store them till the end of the day. He reluctantly agreed. 'You have till 3:15 at the latest to get them out of here, boys.'

Then we hunkered down in the boys' washroom after the bell rang and tried to figure out how to get rid of thousands of fruit flies. This was hard for Farley, cos it meant he was breaking his perfect attendance record.

I wish we'd come up with our last idea first: our last idea was a can of Raid, and it worked.

Our first idea was a vacuum cleaner.

We found one of the janitors in his basement office. He was flipping through a magazine called *The Canadian Fly Fisher*.

'Could we borrow a vacuum?' I asked.

He didn't even look up. 'Bring it back when you're done,' he grunted.

We lugged the vacuum cleaner up two flights of stairs to our lockers. I found an outlet nearby and plugged it in. Farley took off the attachment so that just the nozzle was left. He flipped the switch to ON and held the nozzle in front of him, like a weapon. 'Ready?' he asked.

'Ready,' I replied. Then I opened my locker door and Farley stuck the nozzle inside and sucked up every last fruit fly. We did the same with his locker, too. By then we'd gathered a small crowd of onlookers.

When we were done, a few kids clapped. I'm pretty sure they were being sarcastic. But Farley lapped it up. 'Thank you, thank you, all in the line of duty,' he said, like he was a firefighter who'd just rescued a baby from a burning building.

But our moment of glory was short-lived. Someone shouted, 'They're flying out again!' Sure enough, a bunch of fruit flies were flying *back out of the nozzle that had just sucked them up!!*

Fruit flies are indestructible!!

Farley and I looked at each other, trying not to panic. 'Follow me!' Farley said. So I slapped my hand over the nozzle and followed Farley into the washroom, pulling the vacuum cleaner behind me.

Once we were inside, Farley yelled, 'Give me a loonie, STAT!' like he was a doctor in the middle of a medical emergency. I fished a loonie out of my pocket and handed it to him. I watched, perplexed, as he dropped it into the condom machine.

'What are you doing?' I asked, just as a toilet flushed.

'Yeah, what *are* you doing?' said a familiar voice.

Troy.

Farley shouted, 'I'm buying a condom to put on my nozzle so nothing flies out!'

Yup. He said that. Direct quote.

Troy's eyebrows shot up. For a moment, there was total silence.

Then he burst out laughing. He was laughing so hard, he doubled over. It started to dawn on Farley what he'd just said. 'I meant the vacuum cleaner's nozzle! So fruit flies don't come out!'

Then the strangest thing happened.

Troy patted Farley on the shoulder. 'You crack me up, little man. You and Freckles here.' He started washing his hands. 'How's business going, anyway?'

'Great. We have about two hundred bucks already,' Farley said.

'Wow. A couple of real entrepreneurs,' Troy replied, then he threw an arm around my shoulder, too.

I thought he was going to grab our heads and smash them together. It's what Vlad the Impaler would have done.

But he didn't. He just said, 'See you later,' and walked out of the bathroom.

Farley and I looked at each other, mystified. 'That was weird,' I said.

'Maybe he's trying to turn over a new leaf.'

'Maybe.'

Farley tore open the condom wrapper and rolled the condom over the nozzle of the vacuum cleaner, just like we'd seen our health teacher do with a banana. Then we wheeled the whole thing outside and did our best to empty it.

At lunchtime, we invested some of our hard-earned money on a can of Raid and sprayed our lockers to get rid of any strays.

'Good thinking, fellas,' Troy said from across the hall.

Farley grinned. 'Thanks.'

But I didn't say a word. As far as I'm concerned, the new nicer Troy is *way* creepier than the old jerkface one.

Wednesday, March 27

I'm locked in my bedroom right now, and I am never coming out.

It started at lunchtime. I headed to Mr Jankovich's room with Farley; we were having our final Reach For The Top practice before tomorrow's Provincials in Richmond.

When I walked in, I saw Alberta.

My heart did a little flip. I headed toward her.

'Don't get too close,' she said, putting her hands out in front of her to ward me off. 'I might still be contagious.'

She looked amazing. A little pale, yes, with a greenish hue, but it went well with her outfit. She was wearing plaid polyester pants and her purple Doc Martens and a big oversized T-shirt that read *I'm with Stupid*. The arrow pointed to her left, at Jerome.

'How was your trip?'

'Awful,' I replied.

'Crap. I'm sorry.'

I shrugged. Then she got a funny look on her face, like Dad sometimes gets when he's constipated.

'Henry,' she said, 'I need to tell you something.'

'Shoot.'

'Not here. Let's go out in the hall.'

So I followed her out of the room. I was convinced

she was going to break up with me, even though we weren't officially going out.

'You know how you told me your mom wasn't living with you right now?' she began.

'Yeah,' I said.

'Well, last Thursday, when you were still away and before I got sick? I was walking on Broadway. And I saw your dad, sitting in Blenz. You know, the coffee shop? He was with this blonde woman, and she was holding his hand across the table.'

It felt like someone had put my heart into a vice.

'Was she wearing lots of makeup?' I asked.

'Yup.'

'Did she have . . . ?' I motioned with my hands in front of my chest.

Alberta nodded. 'Big bazongas.'

A group of kids pointed at me and laughed as they walked past. I realized I'd wound up on Alberta's left side, and that the *Stupid* arrow was pointing right at me.

'It was probably nothing,' Alberta said.

But I was already walking away.

'Don't go. Stay for practice,' she called after me.

I didn't turn back. I walked right out of school and all the way home. I called my dad on his cell. I told him it was an emergency and he had to come home right away. I hung up before he could ask any questions.

Ten minutes later, he burst into the apartment, his tool belt still attached to his jeans. 'Henry! Are you OK? What is it? What's happened?'

'You said you wouldn't see Karen while I was gone,' I said. 'You promised.'

It took him a moment to process this. '*This* is why you called me at work?'

'Yes.'

'This is not an emergency—'

'Yes, it is! It's a family emergency!'

'Henry, when I leave work I don't get paid. Do you understand that?'

'My friend saw you. *Holding hands.*'

Dad shook his head. He pulled off his work boots. 'Sit in the living room with me.'

'No.'

'Now!'

So we sat in the living room. 'You lied to me,' I said.

'No, I did not. I promised not to have her in our apartment, and I didn't. But she invited me out for a coffee, and I went. That's all it was, Henry. A coffee.'

'Then why was she holding your hand?' I demanded.

Dad hesitated. 'I told her about Jesse.'

Lucky for me I was sitting down, or I would have toppled over. 'You *what??*'

'Henry, you have no idea what it's like for me—'

'Are you nuts?? It's gonna take, like, five minutes for every single person in this building to find out! They probably already know!!'

'You're wrong. She promised me she'd keep it to herself.'

'And you believed her?? She's a liar, Dad! The first time we met her, she gave us store-bought cookies and said they were homemade!' I stood up and started pacing. 'The whole point about moving here was so we could start over. The whole point was that nobody ever had to find out.'

'Henry, there is nothing wrong with a few people knowing what we've been through—'

'Yes, there is!!! Don't you get it?? They'll look at us different. They'll avoid us. They'll feel sorry for us – or they'll think we're monsters, too! Oh, man, why did you tell her?'

It was Dad's turn to stand up. 'Because she understands! Because there is no one else for me to talk to!' he shouted. 'I can't talk to any of my old buddies in Port Salish; my parents are long dead; and I sure as hell can't talk to my wife!' He slammed his fist against the wall. It went right through the drywall, leaving a big gaping hole. 'Karen's a good listener. And she understands what we're going through, more than you can imagine—'

'Bullshit!' I shouted. 'I hate you!' Then I ran into my room and locked the door, and I've been here ever since.

Dad's tried a couple of times to get me to come out, but I'm not budging, even though I'm starving.

I will stay here all night. I will stay here forever. I will stay here till they have to drag my rotting corpse from the room.

My parents will have two dead kids on their hands.

6:30 p.m.

Unbelievable. Here we are, in the middle of a MAJOR FAMILY CRISIS, and what has my dad just done? He's invited Mr Atapattu in! They're in the living room, watching a hockey game. I just heard Dad tell him, 'Henry's not feeling well.'

LIAR!!! I'm feeling perfectly fine!!!

IT'S YOU WHO'S MAKING ME SICK!!!

8:30 p.m.

I'm starving. My father is letting me starve to death while he and Mr Atapattu talk and laugh and watch the game.

10:00 p.m.

Mr Atapattu finally left. My dad has gone to bed. I just snuck out of my room and went into the kitchen to grab something to eat.

There was a bowl on the counter, filled with one of

Mr Atapattu's curries over rice. It was covered in plastic wrap. Dad had stuck a Post-it Note on top: *Henry, just nuke it for two minutes. Dad xo.*

So I nuked it. I just finished eating it in my room. It was a lamb curry this time, and it was really good. I think my taste buds are getting used to the spices.

At least my hunger is satisfied.

One thing is crystal clear: I'm the only one who's trying to fight for this family.

And I'm beginning to think we may not be worth the fight.

2:00 a.m.

Thanks to my stupid dad and stupid Karen, I am still wide-awake. On tonight of all nights! The Provincials are tomorrow. I need a good night's sleep.

Since I am wide-awake, I am going to write a note.

2:15 a.m.

I just delivered my note. I only had to run up one flight of stairs in my pajamas and slip it under you-know-who's door. This is what it said: *Stay away from my dad. Stay away from our family!!*

Now I'll be able to sleep.

Thursday, March 28

I really thought we could start over. Start fresh. But I was wrong.

Even though I was tired from a crap night's sleep, the day started out great. The whole team piled into a rented van for the ride out to Richmond. Alberta saved a spot for me beside her, but I pretended I didn't notice and sat beside Farley instead. I feel kind of angry with her. I know this sounds stupid, but it's like that saying, 'If a tree falls in the forest and no one hears it, does it make a sound?' If she hadn't seen my dad and Karen together, it would have been like it had never happened. Alberta made it real. And even though I know I shouldn't blame her, I still kind of do.

When we got to the school in Richmond, the parking lot was packed, and groups of kids were heading inside. We were directed into the cafeteria. Tons of teams were there, from all over the province. Imagine the sound of hundreds and hundreds of kids talking and laughing all at once. It was an incredible buzz. Farley kept jumping up and down and saying, 'This is spectacular!'

For a brief moment, I forgot all about the big steaming pile of poop that is the rest of my life, and I let myself get caught up in the energy and excitement. I felt great. I felt happy.

And then I saw Jodie.

Jodie and Jesegan and Parth and Aidan and Ryan and a couple of others I didn't recognize. They were hovering around one of the tables, no more than a hundred meters away.

I froze. My first thought was, *What is she doing here?* Which was followed by, *Of course she's here!* Of course Jodie would be on Port Salish Secondary's Reach For The Top team. This was the girl who'd wanted to be on *Are You Smarter Than a 5th Grader?* as much as I had. And then it dawned on me: we could be competing against them!!

I needed to leave. But, first, I had to look at her one more time. Dumb as it sounds, I needed to see if I could tell how she was doing.

So I peered out from behind Shen's back and gazed at her, trying to look for signs. She looked thinner. And her hair was longer. She was dressed the same as always – in jeans and a pale yellow T-shirt. Yellow is her favorite color.

Then I looked into her eyes at the very moment that she looked into mine. Our gazes locked. Her mouth made a little 'o' of surprise.

She dropped the papers she was holding. Next thing I knew, she was making a beeline for me.

I turned around. Mr Jankovich was checking the schedule to see who we were playing first. 'Sorry, Mr Jankovich. I have to go.'

'What?'

'I feel sick. Barf sick. I have to go.'

'But how will you get home?'

I bolted. I ran out of the cafeteria and out of that school as fast as I could. I found my way to the Canada Line station. I didn't have any money. A nice older lady took pity on me and bought me a ticket.

I'm home now.

When Dad got back from work, I told him what had happened. I thought he was going to lecture me about why I should have stayed. But he didn't. He just went really pale. Then he took a pack of TUMS from his pocket and popped two into his mouth.

I told him I thought we should move to the Yukon. Or, better yet, Newfoundland.

His answer surprised me.

He said he'd think about it.

Which only made me feel worse. Cos I realized he was scared, too.

1:00 a.m.

INTRIGUING FACT: When we're born, we get 50% of our DNA from our mother and 50% from our father. But siblings can still be totally different from each other, because what they get from each parent could be the *exact opposite* 50%.

Sometimes I stare at my face in the bathroom mirror, looking for the DNA Jesse and I shared. We didn't look alike at all. Jesse had dark brown hair like Mom; my hair is vibrantly red, like Dad's. Jesse was tall and skinny like Mom; I'm short and stocky like Dad.

Where I can see Jesse is in my eyes. They're green, with little flecks of brown, big and round. Sometimes I feel like he's looking out of my eyes, seeing what I'm seeing.

Jesse and I saw a lot of things the same way. We laughed at the same jokes. We always picked the same couple to root for on *The Amazing Race*. If Mom and Dad kissed in front of us, we'd both scream, 'Gross!!' And without ever talking about it, we both picked the Great Dane as our favorite wrestler.

And then there are all the ways we were totally different.

But the point is this: no matter how much or how little DNA Jesse and I shared, when people find out you're related to a guy who committed murder/suicide, they can never treat you the same way ever again. They can't help it. Cos they can't help thinking that you are deeply messed up. They can't help thinking that, at any moment, you could go postal, too.

So I know why Dad is scared. I know why I'm scared. We keep trying to run. But we can't seem to hide.

2:30 a.m.

She looked the exact same. A bit taller. A bit thinner.

But other than that? The exact same.

On the outside, anyway.

Sunday, March 31

Dad didn't make me go to school on Friday. He even let me cancel my appointment with Cecil.

I haven't left the apartment all weekend. Dad left once yesterday, to get groceries and a bottle of Jack Daniel's. When Mr Atapattu knocked on our door to watch *Saturday Night Smash-Up*, we pretended we weren't home.

The phone rang a lot yesterday too. I let Dad answer. A couple of the calls were from Mom, but she knows I'm not talking to her. Farley and Alberta called too, but I don't want to talk to them, either.

12:15 p.m.
It's past noon. Dad is still in bed 'sick.' And I've just discovered we are completely out of toilet paper. Dad forgot to buy it yesterday.

I can feel a Number Two coming on.

3:00 p.m.
So I found three dollars and forty-two cents under the couch cushions and went to the corner store. It was barely enough to buy two measly rolls of TP.

On the walk home, it started to pour. I jogged the rest of the way. For the first time in months, I didn't feel breathless, and my wobblies didn't bounce up and down like jelly.

A woman wearing sweatpants and an anorak was struggling to find her keys. She was carrying a bunch of heavy grocery bags. I opened the door for her.

It wasn't till she peeled off her hood that I realized it was Karen.

'Henry,' she said grimly.

She looked different, and it took me a minute to realize I was seeing her without makeup. Her hair hung in wet strands around her face. She had bags under her eyes, and her skin looked gray. She looked like death warmed up.

'Can we talk?' she asked.

'No,' I said. Then, stupidly, instead of making a dash for the stairs, I dashed into the elevator and pressed the CLOSE DOOR button repeatedly. She just followed me inside.

'Fine,' she said, putting down her grocery bags. 'I'll talk, and you listen.' Then she did an unbelievable thing for a grown-up: she pushed me to the back of the elevator and planted herself in front of the doors as they slid shut. We stood staring at each other in the unmoving elevator.

'This is kidnapping,' I said. 'You'd better let me go, or I'll scream.'

She rolled her eyes. 'Like anyone would want to kidnap *you*. Just shut up and listen, and this'll be over before you know it.'

I shut up.

'First I want to say, I'm really sorry about your brother Jesse.'

Hearing her say his name made me want to throw up.

'Believe it or not,' she continued, 'I know how it feels.'

I snorted. 'You don't have a clue—'

'My dad committed suicide when I was fifteen.'

That shut me up again.

'I'm not going to lie to you, Henry. Some of the bad feelings never go away.'

'Gee, great. Thanks for that.'

'Would you rather I lie to you?'

I thought about that for a moment. 'No, I guess not.'

'I just wanted you to know, you're not alone.'

'Yeah, but your dad didn't kill someone else.'

'No. That's a whole other layer of yuck you're going to have to get through.'

'Again. Thanks.'

She shrugged. 'You're already doing way better than me. Nobody got me into therapy, I can tell you that. Drinking was my therapy.'

'Are you a drunk?'

'I prefer the term "alcoholic." Trying to quit again, though. I'm almost two weeks clean and sober.'

Two weeks – big deal, I thought. 'Is that why you look like shit?'

She looked like she wanted to punch me in the face, but all she said was, 'Probably. I *feel* like shit, so it stands to reason.'

I nodded.

'Thing is, I get what your dad is going through. And if he wants to talk, I'm going to listen.'

'What if he wants to do more than talk?'

She looked me right in the eye. 'When you two moved in, I got my hopes up. Your dad's not a bad-looking guy. But, as much as I like him, he's not my type. And now that I know *you* are part of that package . . . *definitely* not interested.'

With that, she turned around and pressed the buttons for our floors. The elevator jerked into motion.

We rode in silence. When the doors opened on the second floor, I stepped out. 'Do you still miss your dad?' I asked.

'All the time,' Karen said. She turned her face away as the doors closed.

Monday, April 1

Dad insisted I go back to school today. 'Just stick with your story,' he said when he dropped me off. 'You were sick.' Then he sat in his truck until he saw me disappear through the front doors.

I saw Ambrose and Parvana in the foyer. 'Are you OK?' Ambrose asked. 'What a lousy time to get sick.'

'I feel better, thanks. How were the Provincials?'

'Awesome!' said Parvana. 'We came in eighth out of thirty teams!' Then she kissed Ambrose right on the mouth, right in front of me. *Get a room*, I wanted to say.

I left them in their lip-lock and headed upstairs. The moment I got to the second floor, I saw Alberta and Farley leaning against my locker. I thought about turning around, but they'd already spotted me. 'What happened, Henry?' Alberta asked as I approached. 'We were worried.' She was wearing her zip-up sweater with the deer on the front.

'We tried calling you all weekend,' Farley added.

'Like I told Mr Jankovich: I was sick. I think it was food poisoning. Undercooked chicken.'

Alberta and Farley shared a look. I could tell they didn't believe me. 'A girl asked after you,' Alberta said.

The vice tightened around my heart.

'She said you used to go to school together,' said Farley. 'She looked disappointed when we said you'd left.'

I didn't say anything. I just shifted a few items around in my locker.

'She asked for your address,' Farley said.

The vice tightened again. I started to see spots in front of my eyes.

'So I gave it to her,' he continued. 'I didn't know your postal code, but she can look that up.'

'You gave her my address?'

'She said she wanted to send you something . . .'

'You told her where I live?'

Farley blinked. 'I hope that's OK.'

I wanted to shout, *No, it's not OK. You stupid idiot, it is not OK!* Instead, I took a deep breath. 'She must have me confused with someone else. I've never seen her before in my life.'

'But, Henry,' Alberta said, 'she knew your name.'

I closed my locker door and walked away.

Much as I wanted to avoid Farley, I couldn't. We had Math together, just before lunch. I sat far away from him, but when the bell rang, he followed me to my locker. 'Henry, I'm sorry I gave that girl your address. I don't know why it made you so angry, but I'm still sorry. I would never do anything to hurt you. You're my best friend.'

I didn't say anything.

'Tomorrow I'm going to bring in all the money we've made so far,' he continued.

'Why would you do that?'

'Because it's enough to buy four tickets, with all the taxes and surcharges and stuff. And we need someone with a credit card to buy them. Maria has one that my parents gave her, but it's only for emergencies. And you want it to be a surprise for your parents . . . So I called my third cousin. He lives near Fraser and 41st. He said he'd order the tickets for us, but I have to bring him the cash first. I'll take the bus there after school tomorrow. You can come, too, if you want.'

'Maybe you shouldn't buy the tickets yet.'

'We have to if we want the best seats. I checked online. They're going fast.'

I took a deep breath. 'I don't think I can go anymore.'

Farley just smiled. 'Ha-ha.'

'I'm serious.'

'But you love the GWF! It's all we've been talking about for months.'

I just shrugged.

'C'mon, Henry. If you don't go, I can't go. And we have the money. Three hundred bucks!'

'Sorry.'

Farley crossed his arms over his scrawny chest. 'I'm bringing in the money anyway and ordering the tickets.

You'll change your mind. I know you will.' Then he walked away, tilting to one side.

That's when I noticed Troy at his locker. He was flipping through a textbook. I wondered how much he'd overheard.

But he didn't even glance my way.

In the afternoon of what was turning into the longest day of my life, I had Home Ec with Alberta.

'We're going to make omelets. The recipe is at your cooking stations,' said Mrs Bardus.

After Farley, Alberta was next in line for people I did not want to see. But I had no choice. We started cracking eggs.

'So,' Alberta said. 'That girl. Was she your old girlfriend or something?' She looked right at me. Well, one eye did.

'Can't you get that fixed?' I said.

'Get what fixed?'

'Your lazy eye. It's totally creepy. Like it has a mind of its own.'

For a brief moment, *both* of her eyes met mine. Her nostrils flared.

Then she cracked the last egg over my head and walked out.

1:00 a.m.

Farley said Jodie wants to send me something. What?? A hate letter? Dog poop? A bomb?

We have *got* to get out of here.

4:00 a.m.

Dad just woke me up from a nightmare. ~~The yellow plastic tube slide one.~~ I was shouting in my sleep.

I'm beginning to think stupid Karen might be right. The bad feelings are never going to go away.

I couldn't face school this morning for a gazillion reasons, but Dad insisted on driving me again. I waved to him as I entered the front doors. I waited thirty seconds. Then I walked back out and came home. I watched *The Price Is Right* and *The View* and a rerun of a really old show called *The Fresh Prince of Bel-Air*.

After that, I walked out of the apartment and took the stairs to the third floor and knocked on Karen's door.

She looked surprised to see me. She was wearing sweatpants again and clutching a mug of tea. Her skin still looked gray. I could hear *The Dr Oz Show* on the TV in her living room.

'Shouldn't you be at work?' I asked.

'It's my day off. Not that it's any of your business.'

She blocked the doorway with her body; she had no intention of inviting me in.

'How did he do it?'

'How did who do what?'

'Your dad.'

'Oh,' she said. 'Carbon monoxide poisoning. Left his car running in our garage.'

'Did you find him?'

'No, my mother did.'

'Did you see his body?'

She gave me a hard stare. Then she stepped away from the door and walked into the living room. I took it as my cue to enter.

Karen's living room is just like ours, except hers is decorated way nicer. Her walls are painted yellow, and it's bright and cheery.

She parked herself in an overstuffed chair and turned off the TV. I sat on her couch.

'No,' she said, 'I didn't. It was a closed casket.'

'I never saw my brother's body, either.'

'Don't you think that was for the best?'

'I don't know. Sometimes I think the pictures in my head might be worse than the real thing.'

She nodded. 'I had those nightmares, too.'

'Had?'

'Had.'

That one little word filled me with relief. Even though I knew her dad had died at least twenty years ago, which meant her nightmares might have stopped only last year, they had still *stopped*.

'Did you . . .' A lump lodged itself in my throat. Karen waited. 'Did you think it was your fault?'

'God, yes.'

'Why?'

'Millions of reasons. I'd been close to my dad when I was younger, but when I got older I thought he was embarrassing. All of his stale jokes and cheap suits. I hated being seen with him. And the last time I saw him, before his death, we had a fight . . . I said some nasty things.'

Neither of us said anything for a moment.

'It took me – it took my family – years to come to terms with the fact that *none of us* was to blame for what my dad did.'

I looked down at my hands.

'You feel guilty about your brother's death, don't you?'

I nodded. And suddenly I was crying. Total waterworks.

Karen immediately got up from her chair. She plunked herself beside me on the couch and put her arms around me and held me tight.

For a brief second, I felt horrified. But then I didn't. I cried and cried and cried, and I'm sure I got snot all over her sweatshirt, but she didn't care. She just held me, and it was like being held by my mom when I was little and had a boo-boo. And next thing I knew, I told her the whole story of The Other Thing that had happened just four weeks before Jesse took Dad's rifle to school. I told the story into her sweatshirt, between great big gulping sobs, and I swear I was back there, smelling the pee smell in the slide, hearing the sound of duct tape, listening to Jesse's screams.

When I was done, she said, 'It is not your fault.' She said it fiercely, into my ear. 'It's not anyone's fault. It took me years of group therapy to finally believe that, Henry, but it doesn't have to take you years. What your brother did was a terrible thing, a genuine tragedy, but it was *his* decision, no one else's.'

'I feel so bad for the Marlins, too. For Jodie.'

'Of course you do. But it is *not your fault*.'

She got up, grabbed a box of Kleenex from her mantel-piece, and shoved it into my hands.

'I used to go to this group. Once in a while, I still drop by if I'm having a bad day. It's for people who've lost someone to suicide. I'd like you to come with me sometime.'

I shook my head. 'I already have a therapist.'

'And I'm sure your therapist is great. But you can do this, too. This is a group of people who've been through it. Nothing you can say about how you've been feeling surprises them, cos they've all felt it, too, in some form or other.'

'But I don't want to talk. I want to forget.'

She snorted. 'You can never forget. Trust me, I drank a lot of booze and took a lot of drugs trying to forget. It's impossible.'

I blew my nose.

'This will be with you forever. But you'll learn to live with it.' She handed me another Kleenex.

'That's the best you can do? *You'll learn to live with it?*'

She nodded. 'Yup. That's the best I can do.'

10:00 p.m.

This is the story I told Karen.

In February last year, Jesse got his first real job at Abdul's Pizza Palace in downtown Port Salish. 'Palace' was an over-statement; the place was just a hole-in-the-wall. In fact, it had an *actual* hole in the wall, made by a drunk guy's fist one night when his Hawaiian pizza took too long. There were no tables; it was strictly a take-out and delivery operation.

Jesse loved that job. Sometimes he'd bring home a pizza that someone hadn't picked up. We'd all tell him how awesome it tasted, and he would actually crack a smile. Abdul was so happy with his work, he increased his shifts and even gave him a fifty-cent-per-hour raise, which made his other two employees jealous because Abdul never gave raises.

Anyway, one night – April 30th to be exact – who comes into the Pizza Palace but Scott Marlin and a few of his friends. And Jesse's alone, or so they think. And they start teasing him, saying stuff like, 'Pizza Face works in a pizza restaurant!' and 'Has anyone ever tried to eat your face?' Then they started bugging him for free pizza.

Jesse refused to give them any freebies, which, when you think about it, was pretty brave cos it was four against one. Finally Scott marched behind the counter and tried

208

to grab a bunch of slices from one of the warming trays, but Jesse blocked his path. Scott easily shoved him out of the way. That's when Abdul came upstairs; he'd been in the walk-in freezer, getting more pizza dough. He started shouting that he was going to call the cops, and Scott and his friends took off.

I only found out that part of the story later, from Abdul.

About an hour after that, I showed up. I'd been at the nine o'clock showing of the last Harry Potter movie with a bunch of friends, including Jodie. My mom and dad were out at a dinner party, and they didn't want me to walk home alone. I told them I'd be fine walking with my friends, but they insisted I meet Jesse at the Pizza Palace so we could walk home together. Looking back, I wonder if it was more for Jesse's sake than for mine.

Jesse gave *me* free pizza. He paid for it out of his own pocket, carefully putting the right amount in the till. I remember I ate an enormous slice of the Heart-Stopper, which was topped with ten different kinds of meat and cheese.

Just after midnight, we said good night to Abdul and started walking home. I remember being glad it was late because no one would see me with my brother.

It was hard for me to write that.

I have to take a break.

10:30 p.m.

OK. To get to our house from Abdul's Pizza Palace took about twenty minutes. But if you cut through the park, it took only ten. Jesse knew my parents wouldn't want us to go through the park after dark.

'C'mon,' I said. 'It's cold out; I'm freezing; we're together; what can happen?'

So we cut through the park.

We'd been walking for only a few minutes when Jesse suddenly said, 'Run.'

I hadn't even heard anything. 'What—' I started.

'Run!' he whispered again, and that's when I heard feet pounding along the ground, getting closer. So I ran. Even though I didn't have any wobblies then, I still wasn't a good runner. I sprinted as far as the playground, which was right in the middle of the park. Then I had to stop to catch my breath.

I turned around. I saw Jesse, also running toward the playground, and, behind him, four figures giving chase.

They were getting closer. I was scared. So I ran up the steps that led to the top of the yellow plastic tube slide, and I launched myself into it. I pressed my arms and legs against the sides and slid slowly down to the bottom, where I stayed, hidden.

But there is a hole in the side of the yellow tube slide.

It's been there forever. I used to toss stones out of it when I was little. I pressed my eye against it.

They were pulling something over Jesse's face. I couldn't tell what it was. I found out later it was a pillowcase.

Then they knocked him to the ground. They took off his shoes. They took off his jeans.

I have to stop again.

11:00 p.m.

Jesse fought them as hard as he could. But it didn't matter that he was a huge GWF fan and knew all the Great Dane's moves; it didn't matter that he'd been lifting weights in the basement for the past year. He'd been ambushed, and it was four against one.

I crouched in the yellow tube slide that smelled of plastic and pee, and I watched as they pulled him to his feet and marched him out of my line of vision.

I inched closer to the bottom of the slide and peered out. They'd pushed my brother against the tetherball pole.

They never said a word, any of them.

Then Scott pulled out a roll of duct tape.

He started tearing long strips off the roll. It made a horrible sound, like nails on a chalkboard. He wrapped the tape around and around Jesse, securing him to the pole.

And then.

I need a minute.

11:45 p.m.

And then they took turns sack-tapping him. Slapping and flicking his testicles, hard.

It went on for what felt like an eternity. Jesse was screaming, the pain was that bad.

I did nothing. I know, I know, what was I supposed to do? I was twelve. I was short. And there was one of me and four of them. But still. Maybe I could have found a stick and snuck up on Scott and his friends and knee-capped them. Or grabbed a big rock and smashed in their skulls.

This is the part that gets to me most, that makes me want to kill Scott even though I know he is already dead: they were laughing. Scott and his friends were laughing. They were trying not to, trying to stay quiet, but I guess they just couldn't help themselves.

After a while, they got bored and walked away, leaving my brother duct-taped to the pole.

What would have happened if I hadn't been there? When would he have been found?

Then again, if I hadn't been there, he never would have taken the shortcut through the park.

I jumped out of the slide. I stumbled over to my

212

brother. I pulled the pillowcase off his head. I used my teeth to rip the strips of duct tape open. I found his shoes and jeans stuffed into a trash can. For a long time, he couldn't even move, the pain was so bad. Finally I helped him into his jeans, and we walked the rest of the way home together. Jesse was hunched over and hobbling like a little old man. I was blubbering like a baby.

But Jesse wasn't. Jesse didn't show a speck of emotion.

Mom and Dad were still out when we got back home. I helped Jesse peel off the rest of the duct tape. It left angry red welts on his skin.

'I should have helped you,' I blubbered. 'I should have killed them.'

'We were outnumbered, Henry. If you'd let them know you were there, they would've hurt you, too.'

'Or they would've run away cos they didn't want a witness,' I said.

'Maybe. I doubt it.'

'We need to call the cops.'

'No.'

'We can take them back and show them where it happened. They can sweep the area for fingerprints.' I'd watched a lot of episodes of *CSI*.

'No,' he said sharply. 'We're not calling the cops.'

'Then we'll tell Mom and Dad—'

'NO!'

He must've seen the look on my face, because he tried to explain. 'If we tell Mom and Dad, they'll make a huge deal out of it. They'll call Scott's parents; they'll call the principal; they'll call the police—'

'Exactly!'

'And at the end of it all, I'll still have to face Scott every time I go to school. And he will find a way to make my life even worse.'

He said all of this calmly, like he was a teacher patiently explaining a math problem.

'No,' I said. 'It doesn't feel right. I want to tell.'

'Henry. Don't.' He looked me in the eye. 'Please.'

So I didn't.

Actually, I did tell one person, sort of.

I told Jodie.

It was a few days later, and we were hanging out at recess. She showed me a new ring she was wearing. 'It's a mood ring,' she told me. 'Scott bought it for me in Gramsimo. He's so sweet.'

'He's an asshole,' I blurted. It just popped right out of my mouth.

Jodie's face turned pink. 'What did you just say?'

'He's a bully, Jodie. He makes my brother's life hell.'

'I don't believe you.' But she hesitated before she said it.

'Ask him. Ask him about last Saturday night,' I said, and I could feel my furies coming on.

'What happened?'

'Ask him!' I shouted.

Then I walked away. I don't know why I lashed out at her; I knew none of this was her fault.

Still, we didn't speak to each other after that.

Four weeks later, both of our brothers were dead.

Here's the worst part: after that night in the park, Jesse actually seemed better. Calmer. He didn't hide out in his room every night. He stopped swearing at my parents. He ate dinner with us and smiled sometimes. Even though Mom and Dad never said anything, I could tell they were relieved. And I was, too.

After IT happened, I felt completely sideswiped. Till I realized Jesse had seemed better because he'd reached a decision. He'd come up with the ultimate solution to all of his problems.

That's why he was calm.

Midnight

After Jesse and Scott were dead – i.e. far too late – I told my parents about that night. They said all the right things. It wasn't my fault; I shouldn't blame myself.

But you know what? I think my mom blames me the

same way she blames my dad. I think she blames us equally. I think she knows she shouldn't, but I think she can't help herself.

I think that is part of the reason why she can't be with us right now. She loves us, but she hates us, too.

Thursday, April 4

The principal called last night and told my dad I'd been skipping for days. Dad was furious. He told me he'd give me one more chance to go back to school on my own, and if that didn't work, he'd come to school with me and sit in on all my classes.

So I went back to school.

My first class was Home Ec. Alberta had a new cooking partner. She acted like I didn't exist. I guess I can't blame her.

My next class was Enriched Math. I wanted to tell Farley I'd still go with him to the *GWF Smash-Up Live!* in Seattle. I've decided that if my mom doesn't come out in time, Mr Atapattu can take her ticket.

But Farley wasn't in Enriched Math.

He wasn't at school all day.

When I got home and called his house, I found out why.

'Oh, Henry,' Maria said when she heard my voice. 'I can't get Farley to come out of his room.' She started to cry.

'What happened?'

'Farley got beat up.'

'I'll be right over,' I said.

I hung up just as Dad got home. I told him what Maria had said. He didn't even take off his coat. 'Let's go.'

We were there in five minutes. Maria let us in. Dad

stayed downstairs with her. I went straight to Farley's room and knocked.

'Farley, it's me. Henry.'

I heard his bed creak. A moment later, he opened the door.

His glasses were broken. One lens was cracked down the middle, and the right arm was held up by Scotch tape. His bottom lip was swollen and cut, and the palms of his hands were badly scraped up.

'What happened?' I asked.

Farley sat on his bed. I perched on his window seat. 'On Tuesday, I brought in all our money, so I could bring it to my third cousin to buy the tickets. I know you said you didn't want to go anymore, but I thought I could change your mind if we actually had *real tickets*, you know? After school, I headed to the bus stop to go to my cousin's place. I walked through one of the laneways.' He paused here and took a deep breath. 'Some guys jumped me from behind. They threw me on the ground, and they went through my jacket pockets. They took all of our money, Henry. All of it.' Fat tears started to roll down his face.

'How many of them were there?'

'I'm not sure. It felt like a lot.'

'Did you see what they looked like?'

Farley shook his head. 'They poked something into my back. They said it was a gun. And they told me not to lift my head for five whole minutes after they left or they'd kill me. Then one of them said, '*Hasta la vista*, sucker,' and they ran away. And I waited because I was scared they might shoot me if I didn't.' He took a hand-kerchief out of his pocket and blew his nose. 'I'm so sorry, Henry. I know you said you didn't want to go anymore, but half of that money was yours.'

'Farley, don't worry about it. Seriously. I'm just glad you're OK.' And the thing is, I really was.

After a while, we went downstairs. My dad insisted we call the cops. I'm sure he was thinking about Jesse in the park that night. I know I was.

A couple of policemen came over, and Farley told them what had happened. The cops were really nice. They wrote out a report, but they said it would be hard to catch the guys responsible after all this time had passed, and that they'd probably already spent the money on drugs.

Maria insisted we stay for dinner, and she let Farley choose because she said he'd barely eaten in the last two days. Farley chose grilled cheese sandwiches with pickles and ketchup, which was an awesome choice.

Afterward, Dad and I drove back home.

I mean it when I say the money doesn't matter to me. It's a bummer after all our hard work, but let's face it: my dream of getting my family back together with a trip to the GWF was doomed to fail anyway.

What worries me is Farley. I saw this look in his eyes when we were there tonight. It was the look Jesse had when Scott threw the Coke can at him. It was a look I'd see on his face over and over again after that, until it just became a part of who he was.

It was the look of giving up.

Monday, April 8

My head is pounding. I just saw twin nurses, but they swear there's only one of them and that I am seeing double.

Not seeing double anymore. Just one nurse. Her name is Sandra. She's kind of cute. It seems I'm in the hospital.

Found my journal in a drawer beside my bed. So tired. This bed is nice. There is a TV above it. *The Ellen DeGeneres Show* is on. Ellen is my mom's favorite.

8:00 p.m.

Speaking of which. I had a dream that my mom was standing above me, squeezing my hand and telling me she loved me.

Must sleep.

Guess what? It wasn't a dream. Mom just walked in with a coffee.

10:00 a.m.

I had to stop writing because when I said hi, she almost dropped her cup. Then she smothered me in a hug. 'Henry, my baby,' she said and practically collapsed on top of me.

When she finally came up for air, I said: 'What are you doing here?'

She just kept crying and said, 'Thank God you're OK. When your dad called and said you had a head injury . . .'

That explains why my head feels like a bowling ball. *How did I get a head injury?* I tried to ask, but my tongue felt thick in my mouth, and she smothered me with another hug.

Now we're watching *Jeopardy!* and trying to shout out the answers before the contestants do, just like the old days. Except that my mind is so fuzzy, I'm doing a lousy job, and I can't shout because, if I do, it feels like a nail gun is shooting into my skull. She tells me Dad's gone home to catch a few hours of sleep. Apparently I've been in here for two days!

I'm so happy she's here. Even if I needed to get a head injury to make it happen. Had I known, I would have tried to get seriously hurt months ago.

Wednesday, April 10

Feeling better today. My head still feels like a watermelon, but I can stay awake for longer than a half hour at a time. Mom's asleep in a chair beside my bed, and Dad has gone to work because, if he doesn't, his boss will 'fire his ass.'

On the windowsill near my bed is a row of cards. One is from Mr Atapattu; another is from Karen. There's even one from Cecil. Mom says he dropped by yesterday, but I was asleep.

Next to the regular-sized cards sits a huge one. It has a drawing of a teddy bear, with red cheeks and a thermometer in his mouth. On the inside, it reads *I can't* bear *to hear you're under the weather.* It's signed *Your friend Farley.* Floating beside the card is a big bunch of brightly colored helium balloons. Mom showed me the card that went with them: It said *Get Well Soon* on the front, and, inside, all of my Reach For The Top teammates had signed it, including Farley again and Mr Jankovich. They all wrote personal messages, too.

Except for Alberta. She just wrote *Alberta.*
Rude.

2:00 p.m.

Here's what I remember:

The morning after I saw Farley, I went to school early

and waited outside for him. When he arrived, he looked even smaller than usual, like he was trying to make himself disappear. He was wearing a pair of glasses that were even uglier than his regular ones. 'We dug out my spares,' he said gloomily. 'It's just till my other ones get fixed.'

For the first time since I'd met him, he wasn't like a rubber ball.

We walked into the school and up the stairs to our lockers in silence. I can play what happened next frame by frame in my head.

Troy was at his locker with his friends Mike and Josh. 'Hey, Fartley, love the new glasses.' They all cracked up. Troy pulled earbuds out of his ears and carefully wrapped them around a new iPod Touch.

A picture flashed through my mind: Troy, standing at his locker, flipping through a textbook, while Farley told me about the money he was going to bring to school the next day.

'You got an iPod Touch,' I said.

'Duh.'

'Where'd you get the money?'

Troy shared a look with Mike and Josh. 'I came into a small inheritance,' he said, smirking. He slid the iPod into his jeans pocket, grabbed a binder from his locker, and closed the door. '*Hasta la vista*, suckers.'

Farley's eyes locked with mine.

Troy started to walk away.

I felt the furies bubble up inside me. 'Can I see it for a sec?' I heard myself saying. 'I'm thinking of getting one myself.'

Troy considered my request. 'You can look,' he said, pulling it out of his back pocket, 'but don't touch. I don't want your germs on it.' He held it out in the palm of his hand.

I moved in for a closer look. Then I grabbed it and ran like hell.

Next thing I remember, I woke up in hospital.

5:00 p.m.

Dad filled in a couple of blanks when he came by after work. 'I got a call at the construction site just after 9:00 a.m. It was your principal. He said you'd fallen and hit your head, and that you'd been taken to the hospital in an ambulance. I didn't even tell my boss where I was going. I just tore out of there and drove to the hospital.

'The doctor told me you'd suffered a concussion and they were keeping you under observation because they wanted to make sure there was no bleeding on the brain.'

My dad had to stop for a moment to compose himself. 'Bleeding' and 'brain' were two words he'd heard a lot after Jesse did what he did.

'Then the principal showed up, and all he could tell me was that you'd been in a fight and hit your head. He still didn't know all the details, but he said a friend of yours got help immediately and the ambulance was there very fast. I called your mom, and she caught the first flight. You had us terrified there for a while, Henry.'

Now both my mom and my dad are sitting beside my bed. Mom's sleeping, and her head is resting against Dad's shoulder. He's holding her hand.

And even though I may have a brain injury, I haven't felt this content in a really long time.

6:30 p.m.
Mystery solved.

Farley came by after school and filled in the rest of the blanks. His lip was almost back to normal. He was wearing his regular glasses again.

'Greetings, Mrs Larsen,' he said when he met my mom. 'I've been looking forward to meeting you.' Then he bowed low and kissed her hand. Mom raised an eyebrow at me, but she was smiling. Since I had company, she decided to go home and have a shower, which was probably a good thing because her hair was starting to look greasy.

Farley was like a hummingbird, darting around the room, checking everything out. He pressed the buttons on my bed to make it move up and down. Then he pressed the button that called the nurses' station.

'Oh. Sorry. I was just seeing if it worked,' he said to Sandra when she entered.

'Henry, keep an eye on your friend,' Sandra said, winking at me.

She's my favorite.

'There's so much to tell you!' Farley exclaimed as he finally sat down in the chair next to my bed. 'Troy's been expelled!'

'What??'

'Well, not expelled, schools can't really do that anymore, but he was "strongly encouraged" to change schools. It turns out they've had a file on him all along. A *big* file, going all the way back to when he put that peanut in Ambrose's sandwich.'

That made me wonder if Port Salish Secondary had had a file on Scott all along. Maybe Jesse should have given them more credit.

'Wait – back up. What happened? The last thing I remember is grabbing his iPod.'

Here's what Farley told me:

Apparently I ran into the boys' washroom. Troy was so startled, it took him a moment to chase after me. By the time he, Mike, Josh, and Farley had burst into the washroom, I was already standing in one of the stalls.

And I'd already thrown Troy's iPod Touch into the toilet. And I'd already started flushing repeatedly.

Apparently I also started talking Robot. 'You. Are a Dick,' I said to Troy. 'A Jerk. A Creep. A Waste. Of Space.'

Farley says Troy screamed a whole pile of words I can't repeat, then he ordered me to get his iPod out of the toilet.

So I did. I scooped it out of the toilet bowl, but instead of handing it back to him, I threw it onto the hard tile floor and started stomping on it.

That's when Troy began punching me. Farley says I got in a couple of not-bad swings myself. 'But the best part was when you tried to do the Bell Clap.' The Bell Clap is one of the Great Dane's favorite moves, and it involves slapping both ears of your opponent really hard with the palms of your hands to distort their balance.

I groaned.

'Yeah, it didn't do much,' Farley admitted. 'It only made him angrier. But it *looked* cool.'

Apparently it was after I attempted the Bell Clap that Troy punched me so hard, I fell back and hit my head on the toilet seat and blacked out.

'That was scary,' Farley said. 'You just crumpled. You lay there on the bathroom floor, not moving. Troy freaked. He and Mike and Josh just cleared out. I was shouting at you to wake up, and then Ambrose came into the bathroom, and I told him to go get the principal, and I pulled out my cell phone and called 911.'

'Thanks, Farley. You pretty much saved my life.'

'I pretty much did!' he gloated.

He left his chair and perched on the edge of my bed. 'While we were waiting for the ambulance,' he said, 'you came to for a while. But you were totally disoriented. You kept talking about someone named Jesse.' Farley looked at me with his magnified eyes. 'Who's Jesse?'

I took a deep breath. Then I did what was either the bravest thing I've ever done or the stupidest.

'He's my brother,' I said.

And then I told Farley the whole horrible truth.

When I was done, Farley was really quiet. His glasses had fogged up. I couldn't tell what he was thinking.

'I'll understand if you don't want to hang around me anymore,' I said.

He took off his glasses and wiped the lenses on his pants. 'Why would I not want to hang around you?'

I shrugged. 'It freaks people out. Like they think our whole family has cooties or something.'

Farley put his glasses back on. 'Henry, what you did for me the other day – you were like the Great Dane, taking on Vlad the Impaler. You defended me against the ultimate heel.'

He took his handkerchief from his pocket and blew his nose. 'You're my best friend in the whole world.'

I looked at him, sitting on my bed. I took in his magnified eyes, his pocket protector, his pants that were buckled right under his nipples.

And I said, 'You're my best friend, too.'

Then my eyes got a bit moist, and Farley opened his arms, and I realized he was coming in for a hug. It was turning into way too much of a Hallmark Moment. Luckily an aide brought in my supper tray just before he could swoop in, and he got distracted. '*Ooh*, is that Salisbury steak? Are you going to eat it?' he asked me.

It looked disgusting – a piece of dry meat with congealed gravy on top. 'No,' I said. 'Dad's bringing me an individual pizza from Panago.'

'May I?'

I laughed. 'Go for it.'

Farley dug right in. He ate every last bite. I sat propped up in my bed and watched him, amazed that I had ever dreamed of getting an upgrade, when I'd had the best model all along.

I wish I could say that things went as well with Alberta as they did with Farley, but they didn't.

She finally came by this morning, carrying a plastic container full of muffins. 'I made them myself,' she said as she sat in the chair beside my bed. 'Blueberry.'

I took one out and ate it. It was quite good, and I only had to pull one unidentifiable crunchy thing out of my mouth.

'Thanks,' I said when I was done. 'Delicious.'

She just looked down at her purple Doc Martens, and it dawned on me that she was embarrassed to let me see her eyes.

'I'm really sorry for what I said to you that day, Alberta—'

'You should be,' she interrupted. 'It was cruel.'

'I know. I guess I was trying to be cruel. I was scared.'

'Scared of *what*?'

'That you'd find out the truth.'

'About what? About that girl?'

I nodded. 'Yes, sort of. About her, and her brother. And my brother.'

'The one who died of cancer?'

I sighed. After being silent on the subject for so long, here I was, having to tell the story two days in a row. 'About that,' I began.

• • •

When I was done, Alberta was completely silent. Tears were rolling down her face. I didn't mean to make her cry, but let's face it: it's a sad story.

She stood up and leaned over me. I really thought she was going to kiss me, and I was worried about my breath because I hadn't brushed my teeth, and I knew I must have horrible morning stinks.

But she didn't kiss me.

She punched me in the stomach.

'You lied to me,' she said.

Then she punched me again, one for the road before she stormed out.

Friday, April 12

The doctors say I can go home today. I'm not allowed to go back to school yet; they want me to rest at home for at least a week and come back in for a checkup. Then they'll decide if I'm ready. This is fine by me.

I told Sandra she could have the balloons. She gave me a hug and told me to stay out of trouble. I said I'd try my best.

1:00 p.m.

I'm in my room now, resting.

I thought it would feel good, coming back to the apartment with both my parents. But to be honest, it's weird.

First we had to walk past new handwritten signs in the foyer. The first one read WE SHOULD NOT HAVE TO GET RID OF YOUR JUNK MAIL!! PLEASE DEAL WITH IT YOURSELF!! The second note, stuck underneath the first one, read GET A LIFE!!!!!

Then, when we entered the apartment, I saw the photos. Mom had obviously been down in the storage locker, because there were at least ten framed pictures of Jesse, or Jesse and me, or Jesse, me, Mom and Dad, hanging on the living-room walls.

And Jesse was there, too.

The shoebox was sitting on the mantelpiece above the gas fireplace. My mom must've seen me staring at it because she said, 'I can't believe your father's had him under his bed all this time.'

'At least I was with him,' my dad retorted, and my stomach lurched because I knew right then and there that they'd been fighting a lot.

Then my dad picked up a bubble envelope from the hall table and handed it to me. 'This arrived for you when you were gone.'

I knew the handwriting immediately.

Jodie. Her name was written in the left-hand corner, with an address I didn't recognize.

My knees suddenly didn't want to support me. I almost fell over right there in the hall.

'Do you want us to read it first?' my mom asked. They both looked worried.

I shook my head. But I didn't open it.

I still haven't opened it. It's sitting on my bedside table.

After IT happened, a lot of my friends made it clear they were no longer my friends. It happened to my parents, too. I had to shut down my hotmail account and my Facebook page, thanks to a few death threats.

Then there was the night someone started a fire in our garage.

So it's not surprising that I'm afraid to open a letter

from the sister of the boy Jesse killed, even if she was once my best friend in the whole wide world.

2:30 p.m.
I can't stand it anymore. I'm opening it.

April 4

Dear Henry,

I've tried e-mailing you a couple of times, but they always bounce back. I was starting to think I would never find you again. So when I saw you at the Provincials, it was so weird. It was like I was seeing a ghost. When you vanished into thin air, I thought maybe I HAD seen a ghost. But then I talked to some of the kids on your team, and I knew you were real.

You saw me, too, didn't you? And you didn't want to talk to me. Maybe you haven't even told your friends what happened. I wouldn't blame you. I saw how people treated you and your family afterward. I rode past your house the day after your garage was lit on fire. Not because I was gawking, but because I thought I might see you.

Everything is so horrible, Henry. It's like a nightmare, except I never wake up. And nobody gets it; nobody really understands, not even my grief counselor. And my parents are so messed up. My dad has a lot of hate. He doesn't know I'm writing to you; he'd be furious if he did. My sister, thankfully, is too young to get it. But I know that the one person who will totally GET IT is you. Cos you're living through the same nightmare, am I right? Maybe even worse.

I have so many questions I would ask you if I could. Do you have more bad days than good? Are your parents as totally messed up as mine? Do you have nightmares? Do you sometimes hate your brother? I sometimes hate Scott, and then I feel so bad, I want to hurt myself.

I wish you still lived here, Henry. Even though I know you never could.

Well, anyway . . . I really don't know what else to say. Please, please write back, but not to my house, OK? You could write to Carrie's house – she won't tell anyone. Her address is on the envelope.

Bye for now, Henry.
Jodie

PS – I really hope you write back.
PPS – I hope you like the gift.

I read the letter three times in a row. Then I tipped the envelope and eased out a small, flat object that was carefully wrapped in layers of Bubble Wrap.

It was our sand dollar. The perfect sand dollar we'd found on the beach a couple of years ago. I am holding it in my left palm right now. It is cool and smooth.

I'd let her keep it because she'd been having a bad day. I guess she's returning the favor.

Sunday, April 14

Mr Atapattu came over yesterday. He was carrying a gift-wrapped box. 'Henry, I am so glad to see that you are alright,' he said. He handed me the box. 'For your recovery. Straight from the Home Shopping Network.'

I tore off the wrapping paper. Inside was my very own Slanket, in navy blue. 'Thanks,' I said as I slipped it on. It felt like I was wrapped in a cocoon.

Mr Atapattu picked up a framed photo from the mantelpiece. It was a picture of me, Jesse, and Mom, standing in front of the Legoland sign.

'That's my brother,' I said.

'Yes, I know.'

'Did Dad tell you what happened?'

'No.'

'Karen?'

He shook his head. 'I've known for a long time. I Googled you shortly after you moved in.'

I raised my eyebrows, but he just shrugged.

'After you've had a meth lab next door, you tend to do your research.'

'So you've known this whole time?'

'Yes.'

'And you still wanted to get to know us. You were still nice to us.'

'You sound surprised.'

I was. I was also near tears. I blame my head injury.

'Henry, when tragedy befalls someone, it is when he needs comforting most.'

'I just thought you were a lonely old man, desperate for company,' I blurted.

Again, I blame my head injury.

But he just laughed. 'Oh, I'm definitely that, too. It wasn't entirely unselfish, I assure you.'

He could see I was starting to get tired, so we turned on the TV. Dad had PVR'ed a bunch of GWF shows while I was in hospital. We started watching *Monday Night Meltdown*, and, at the first commercial break, an ad came on for the *GWF Smash-Up Live!* in Seattle! 'Tickets are going fast! Get yours now to avoid disappointment!'

'I was *this close* to going to that show,' I told him.

'Really?'

I nodded. And even though I was tired, I wound up telling Mr Atapattu the whole story about Recycling Managerial Services and Farley getting robbed and my fight with Troy.

'That's terrible,' he said. 'Did you know I was robbed three times when I drove my cab?'

'Seriously?'

'It was very frightening.'

'I bet.' I was starting to feel dozy in my Slanket.

'*The GWF Smash-Up Live!* in Seattle,' I heard him say. 'That would have been quite an experience.'

Then I didn't hear anything else because I fell asleep.

This morning Dad asked if it was OK if him and Mom went for a walk. I said sure. Once they were gone, I headed upstairs to Karen's apartment.

'Hey,' she said when she opened the door. 'You're back.' Her hair was freshly washed, and she was wearing jeans and a sweater.

'You look different,' I told her.

'How so?'

'Better. Not so tired. Or so slutty.'

'Watch your mouth.'

'I meant it as a compliment.'

'To be honest, I feel like crap. But I'm almost a month sober.'

'Congratulations.'

She let me in and made me a peanut butter and jelly sandwich. We sat together in her living room.

'Did you hate him?' I asked.

She knew exactly what I meant. 'I did. For years. But now . . . I just have compassion. Dad would never have intentionally hurt us, you know? His depression must have been crushing him to do what he did.'

I can hardly believe I'm writing this, but it's true: Karen

is so easy to talk to. She's been there. And she just tells it like it is.

'Do you still think about him a lot?'

'Every day. But they're almost all nice thoughts now. They're memories of the good times. Because we had a lot of good times before he took his life. Did you and your brother have a lot of good times?'

'Yeah. I guess so.'

'Then put your energy into remembering that,' she said. 'You're the keeper of your brother's memory. He did an awful thing, Henry. But he wasn't an awful person.'

5:00 p.m.

I'm in my room now. Mom's cooking a roast chicken for dinner. The apartment has never smelled so good.

I'm looking through a photo album. It's one of a stack Mom brought up from the storage locker. There's a picture of Jesse and me, when he was nine and I was seven, sitting outside a pup tent in our backyard. We're wearing our pajamas, and we're laughing hard.

I remember that morning so well. It was the first time Mom and Dad let Jesse and me sleep in the backyard in the tent. Jesse had pleaded for most of that summer, and Mom finally said OK. Dad helped us pitch the tent, and we filled it with sleeping bags and pillows and flashlights and a bunch of comic books and snacks.

We had a ton of fun, until it got dark. Then I got scared. The wind rustled through the trees, and I was sure there were black bears or monsters coming to get us. I started to cry. I wanted to go inside.

Jesse didn't call me a sissy or a baby. He talked to me in a calm voice. He'd just finished reading a book called *The BFG*, and he started to tell me the story. It was about a girl named Sophie, who befriends a Big Friendly Giant. It was an amazing tale about capturing good dreams to give to children and battling a band of very *un*friendly giants. Next thing I knew, it was morning: I'd slept through the night in the tent.

'You did it,' he said when we both woke up at the crack of dawn, thanks to a woodpecker that was tapping on a nearby tree.

'I did!' I replied.

Jesse high-fived me. We unzipped the tent and saw Mom, peering anxiously out of her bedroom window. We waved. She and Dad made us a huge pancake breakfast.

That's a good memory.

It's a start.

Wednesday, May 1

1:00 a.m.

You'll never guess where I am.

I am in the backseat of a rented minivan. Mom and Karen are in the middle row, chatting. Dad is sitting beside Mr Atapattu, who is driving. Farley and Jesse are with me in the backseat. We're heading home after the most awesome night of my life.

Here's how it happened. Farley showed up at our apartment this morning at nine o'clock. Normally I wouldn't even be out of bed, but Mom and Dad had woken me up at eight, with the excuse that Mom had made a big breakfast, which she didn't want to go to waste.

'What are you doing here?' I asked him.

'Your parents invited me to breakfast,' he said, and maybe it's the lingering effects of the concussion, but I didn't even stop to think that this was weird.

Then Mr Atapattu showed up. He was grinning, showing off his very white teeth. 'Henry, will you help me with something downstairs?' he said.

By then I was starting to get suspicious, especially when everyone else came downstairs, too. The minivan was waiting out front. Karen was standing beside it. 'Get in,' Mr Atapattu said.

'Where are we going?' I asked.

'Seattle,' said Mr Atapattu.

My eyes widened. 'No way. No way no way no way!'

'It's true, it's true!' Farley shouted, grabbing my arms and jumping up and down.

'You told me about the surprise you'd been planning for your parents,' Mr Atapattu said. 'So we decided we'd turn the tables and plan a surprise for *you*.'

I could feel my eyes start to sting, and I had to dig my fingernails into my palms. 'Thank you,' I said.

Mr Atapattu shrugged. 'It was either spend some money on this trip, or spend it on some very expensive vitamin supplements I saw on the Home Shopping Network.'

We all piled into the van. Mr Atapattu put the key in the ignition. And suddenly I pictured Jesse, sitting on the mantelpiece. He'd loved the GWF more than anyone. Even in his darkest days, he would sit with the rest of us and watch *Saturday Night Smash-Up*.

I couldn't leave him by himself on today of all days.

'I forgot something,' I said just as Mr Atapattu was about to pull away.

So I ran back upstairs and brought down the shoebox. Mom started to protest: what if the van got broken into, what if the border guards asked questions? But Dad squeezed her hand, and she took a deep breath, and I climbed into the back with my brother.

We had so much fun in Seattle. We arrived at lunchtime, and it was a sunny day, so we ate our sandwiches outside before going up the Space Needle. Later on, we visited the Pike Street Market. Then it was time to hit the stadium.

I was worried that they wouldn't let Jesse in. I'd slipped him into my backpack, and security guards were checking everyone's bags. But when the security guards looked into mine, all he said was, 'New shoes?'

'Yes,' I lied. He waved me through.

It was an awesome night. Our seats were good, in the thirtieth row. They had big-screen TVs so you could see everything up close and personal. Farley had even brought homemade signs to wave. His said VLAD THE IMPALER IS #1! Mine said THE GREAT DANE IS #2! Farley thought that was hilarious.

My mom was thrilled when El Toro hit the ring. Best of all, he had a rematch with Jack Knife, and this time El Toro whipped his butt. He flipped Jack Knife right over the ropes and out of the ring! And my dad went mental when the Twister took on the Thompson Twins and won.

At the break, Karen took us to one of the shops in the stadium and said, 'You can each spend fifty bucks.'

'We can't spend your money—' I started.

'Yes, we can!' said Farley as he raced into the shop.

'Suresh Atapattu isn't the only one who can treat his friends,' Karen said to me. She'd sat beside Mr Atapattu on the way down, which was a big mistake. They'd argued about everything: his driving, which lane to choose at the border, which route to take into the city, where to park when we arrived. So if she needed us to spend her money to even out some invisible playing field, who was I to argue?

Farley bought a Vlad the Impaler T-shirt and a Vlad the Impaler poster. I bought a Great Dane hoodie and lunch box. I told Karen why I wanted the lunch box. 'Do you think your parents will approve?' she asked.

I shrugged. 'It's better than a shoebox.'

The second half of the show was even better than the first, especially when the Great Dane hit the ring. I went nuts. And guess who his opponent was? Vlad the Impaler! Farley and I both went nuts!! (And so did my dad, which was a little embarrassing. Grown men really shouldn't pump their fists in the air and go, '*Whoooooooooooo!*')

It was a spectacular match. Best of all, the Great Dane won! And he did it with no underhanded tricks or illegal moves (although he did rub his butt in Vlad's face when he was lying on the mat, groaning in defeat, but, really, who could blame him?).

For tonight, at least, the underdog won.

• • •

I went to my session with Cecil last Friday. He looked pretty happy to see me. I told him the story I told Karen. I told him without once using Robot-Voice. He said he was proud of me for sharing such a painful memory.

I also told him about Jodie, and the letter. I even brought in the sand dollar and let him hold it.

'Holy Moly,' he said. 'It's so smooth.'

Then he helped me write a letter to her. He actually had a lot of good advice. He even gave me a stamp.

When it was time for me to go, he said, 'By the way, I've watched a couple episodes of *Saturday Night Smash-Up*.'

'And?'

'It's pretty addictive,' he said.

He still needs a haircut. And new socks. But other than that? Cecil's not such a bad guy.

Going back to school was hard.

Farley met me at the front doors on my first day. 'I think word's leaked out.'

'About . . . ?'

'About your brother. They didn't hear it from me,' he added quickly. 'Or Alberta. But you were talking about your brother in the bathroom . . . Maybe someone looked it up on the web?'

Barf. 'How do you know people know?'

'A couple of kids have asked me about it. Ambrose asked me yesterday.'

'And what did you say?'

'I said he should ask you.'

I sighed. 'Gee, thanks.'

We entered the school. I could tell right away from the looks I got that Farley was right. People knew. But I think Farley must've talked to the Reach For The Top kids because, whenever I walked into a classroom, one of them would come and sit beside me right away. Like in Socials, Jerome sits beside me all the time now. He's a man of few words. 'Hey,' he'll say as he slips into the seat beside me.

'Hey,' I'll say back.

In Enriched English, Farley, Ambrose, and Parvana form a little triangle around me. In Enriched Math, Farley and Shen flank me on either side. It's a little obvious, but you know what? It's also appreciated. And after just two weeks, I notice that the glances and whispers are starting to ease up.

I asked Dad to drive me to Alberta's house the day before I started back at school. Cricket answered the door.

'Alberta, it's that guy you sucked face with!' she shouted before running upstairs.

Rude.

Alberta came to the door. She scowled when she saw

me. She was wearing a short-sleeved, red-and-white checked shirt, like a cowgirl would wear, over thick black tights.

'I like your shirt,' I said. 'Value Village?'

She just kept scowling at me.

'Alberta,' I said. 'I'm sorry, about everything. I'm sorry I lied. I was scared you might not like me anymore if I told you the truth.'

She crossed her arms over her chest. 'I forgive you,' she said. 'But if you ever lie to me again . . .'

'I won't.'

'Good.'

Things are still a little awkward between us. But I called her on my cell phone from the van this morning anyway, to tell her where I was going.

'Cool,' she said. Then, just before she hung up: 'Hey, Henry. How many wrestlers does it take to screw in a lightbulb?'

'I don't know.'

'Duh, what's a lightbulb?' There was a pause, followed by '*Ha-ha-ha-ha-ha-ha-HEEE-haw!*'

I'd like to say that everything is good between my parents, but that would be a lie. They argue, a lot. They try to keep their voices down, but I hear them. Sometimes I escape to Karen's or Mr Atapattu's, just so I can breathe.

I have to be really careful about what I say around

Mom. A few nights ago she was making supper, and a song I liked came on the radio. I started to say 'This band is killer,' but I stopped myself just in time and said, 'This band is kil . . . ometers better than all the other bands out there.' And I rarely play on the PS3 anymore because most of the games involve shooting, which upsets her too much.

It's still better having her here than not. But it isn't great. Mom says she needs to go back to Picton soon – to get a bunch of stuff and wrap up her sessions with Dr Dumas. She says she's coming back, but I don't totally believe her.

I'm not sure how my parents will feel when I tell them I'd like to move Jesse's ashes into the Great Dane lunch box. It doesn't have to be forever, but it's a big step up from the shoebox. And I think Jesse would like it.

On Monday I'm going to a suicide bereavement support group with Karen. She's convinced me to go just once, to see what it's like. Cecil seemed really pleased when I told him about it. Going with Karen makes it seem doable.

Today was a very good day. Tomorrow might not be so good. The anniversary of IT will be awful. The dread has been building inside me for weeks.

But I also know that life goes on.

Which reminds me.

I'm going to have to ask Cecil for a new notebook.

Q&A with Susin Nielsen

Why did you choose to write this particular story?
The idea came to me when I was reading a book by Wally Lamb, called *The Hour I First Believed*. He'd put one of his characters into the very real-life tragedy of the Columbine High School shootings. There was a line in the book that just gutted me; he mentioned that one of the shooters had a brother (this is a fact; I followed up with a lot of my own research). I couldn't get that out of my head. I'd never thought about the surviving family members of a kid who commits a horrible act of violence. That's how Henry was born: I just started thinking about the brother who is left behind. Jesse was nothing like those Columbine shooters, of course; his circumstances were very different.

This is a darker novel than your first two. Was that more of a challenge? Did it worry you at all?
I would say it was more of a challenge in the sense that I had to go to a darker place. But I was determined the book would still have a lot of humor, because it's from Henry's perspective and a lot of what he says and observes is (usually inadvertently) funny. I simply could not write a book without humor. But I also knew I was going out

on a creative limb; I had no idea if people would respond favorably to that blend of dark and light.

You often have a theme or thread of bullying in your novels. Why?

Good question. I never set out to write about an issue, that's for sure. I just try to find interesting characters and put them into interesting situations. That said, I do love an underdog, and all of my protagonists fall into that category. They need obstacles and people who make their lives difficult. In *Word Nerd*, Ambrose is a bit of a bully magnet. In *Dear George Clooney, Please Marry My Mom*, Violet gets teased by two girls at school. And in this novel, Henry isn't picked on a lot, but his brother was tormented terribly, and then he sees Farley getting it, too. And of course he chooses to stand up to them, at his own peril.

Speaking of Farley, he's a wonderful character, as is Alberta. How did you come up with them?

I love Farley and Alberta. I wanted Farley to first come across as a bit of a stereotype in Henry's eyes; then, over time, he comes to realize what an amazing human being Farley is, and what a great friend. Who wouldn't want Farley on their side? And Alberta, oh I just love her too. I love writing girls who aren't girly-girls. I was in a seminar once with a bunch of teens and someone complimented one of the girls on her clothes, and she said, 'Thanks. I call it the recycled look.' And that just twigged for me. I knew I wanted to have a female character who dressed like that, and who came with a lot of attitude, but also a lot of vulnerability underneath.

Was it a special challenge to write in journal form?
Yes!!! For many reasons. First of all, some would say journal format has been done to death. So I knew I had my work cut out for me. Second, all my books have been in first person, but a journal was really different. I could only write about things *after they'd happened*, because that's how diaries work! I couldn't write as things were unfolding, which I've been able to do in my other novels.

The fictional Global Wrestling Federation plays a big part in the book. Why?
I needed something unique for Farley and Henry to bond over. Also, I loved the metaphorical aspect of 'babyfaces' and 'heels,' and how Henry could relate that to his brother.

Are you a wrestling fan?
No, not in the slightest! But I did a lot of research: I

watched a lot of WWE shows and even bought a very expensive coffee table book on all the WWE wrestlers, to look at how they broke down their stats and skills, etc. Oh, and I read Bret Hart's autobiography, *Hitman*.

Acknowledgements

I've never met author Wally Lamb, but it was a line in his book *The Hour I First Believed* that inspired me to write this story. I thank him from afar. I also read and enjoyed Bret Hart's book *Hitman*, which gave me good insight into the world of professional wrestling.

For their expertise and time, I must thank Chris Matisz, the Reach For The Top coach at Kitsilano Secondary School; Catherine MacMillan, counselor extraordinaire at Kitsilano Secondary School; Constable Lindsey Houghton, media relations officer with the Vancouver Police Department; Gordon Kopelow for his expert advice on all things legal; and Laurie Hollingdrake, a gifted therapist. Thanks also to Ian Weir for a good wrestling joke.

I also want to thank my early readers for their extremely helpful feedback: Göran and Oskar Fernlund, Robin Fowler, Sam Woodbridge, Susan Juby, and all of the bibliophiles from Christianne Hayward's Lyceum.

Then there are the usual suspects: my wonderful agent, Hilary McMahon, and the entire team at Tundra, with special thanks going to Kathryn Cole, who, along with Sue Tate, championed my manuscript; my fantastic editor, Sue Tate; Tara Walker, for her valuable suggestions; Kelly Hill, for another wonderful cover; Pamela Osti, my terrific publicist; and Kathy Lowinger, without whom

I would not have found such a happy home at Tundra.

And last but far from least: a very special thank you to Seve Williams. Seve will probably one day rule the world, but in the meantime, he generously let me use his recycling for profit/fruit fly story, and for that I am eternally grateful.

WE ARE ALL MADE OF MOLECULES

A NOVEL BY SUSIN NIELSEN

Meet Stewart. He's geeky, gifted but socially clueless.
His mom has died and he misses her every day.

Meet Ashley. She's popular, cool but her grades are no good.
Her dad has come out and moved out – but not far enough.

Their worlds are about to collide: Stewart and his dad are
moving in with Ashley and her mom. Stewart is trying to be
89.9% happy about it even as he struggles to fit in at his new
school. But Ashley is 110% horrified and can't get used to her
totally awkward home. And things are
about to get a whole lot more mixed up
when these two very different people
attract the attention of school hunk
Jared . . .

'Susin Nielsen is one of the best writers
working today' *Susan Juby*

9781783442324   Hardback £12.99

GOODBYE STRANGER
Rebecca Stead

Bridge has always been a bit of an oddball, but since she recovered from a serious accident, she's found fitting in with her friends increasingly difficult. It's getting harder to keep their promise of no fights, especially when they start keeping secrets from each other.

Sherm wants to get to know Bridge better. But he's also hiding a secret.

And then there is another mystery girl, who is struggling with an even more serious friendship problem. . .

Told from interlinked points of view, this is a bittersweet story about the trials of friendship and growing up.

'Superb' *Kirkus*, starred review

'Immensely satisfying'
School Library Journal,
starred review

9781783443994 £7.99 paperback

REBECCA STEAD

**WINNER OF THE GUARDIAN CHILDREN'S FICTION PRIZE
AND SHORTLISTED FOR THE CARNEGIE MEDAL**

When Georges moves into a new apartment block
he meets Safer, a twelve-year-old self-appointed
spy. Soon Georges has become his spy recruit. His
first assignment? To track the mysterious Mr X,
who lives in the flat upstairs. But as Safer becomes
more demanding, Georges starts to wonder: what
is a game and what is a lie?
How far is too far to go for
your only friend?

'A joy to read' *Independent*

'Rebecca Stead makes
writing this well look easy'
Philip Ardagh, Guardian

9781849395427 £6.99 Paperback

A YEAR IN THE LIFE OF A TOTAL AND COMPLETE GENIUS

STACEY MATSON

I, Arthur Bean, am going to be famous. It's not going to be easy, I know. The teachers don't understand my creative brilliance. My true love, the beautiful Kennedy, barely notices me. Plus Robbie Zack (what a loser) thinks that I steal his ideas, which I don't. I just need to win the story-writing contest this year . . .

Welcome to the mind of Arthur Bean, genius. Life hasn't been easy for him, but he's going to make it all right with his brilliant stories. Only problem is, what he writes often gets him into big trouble . . .

Through letters, doodles, email exchanges and 'SEE ME' notes enter the funny, touching and often mixed-up mind of Arthur Bean, creative genius.

'Brings to mind Jeff Kinney's hilarious *Wimpy Kid*'
Books for Keeps

9781783443017 £6.99 paperback